THE FREE

Move the Mountains

EMILY CONOLAN

ALLEN&UNWIN

SYDNEY · MELBOURNE · AUCKLAND · LONDON

First published by Allen & Unwin in 2019

Allen & Unwin
83 Alexander Street
Crows Nest NSW 2065
Australia
Phone: (61 2) 8425 0100
Email: info@allenandunwin.com
Web: www.allenandunwin.com

A catalogue record for this book is available from the National Library of Australia

ISBN 978 1 76029 494 6

For teaching resources, explore
www.allenandunwin.com/resources/for-teachers

Cover design by Karen Scott and Sandra Nobes
Text design by Sandra Nobes and Karen Scott
Set in 11.5 pt Sabon by Sandra Nobes
Vintage map on pages 278–279 © Lukasz Szwaj/Shutterstock
and NZ map © dikobraziy/Shutterstock
Photo of Emily Conolan on page 284 © Nick Tompson
This book was printed in Australia in June 2019 by McPherson's Printing Group

10 9 8 7 6 5 4 3 2 1

The paper in this book is FSC® certified. FSC® promotes environmentally responsible, socially beneficial and economically viable management of the world's forests.

www.emilyconolan.com.au

To my Zia Rosella, for all the energy
you have given this book. Grazie mille!

WARNING: YOU MAY DIE
WHILE READING THIS BOOK.

When you read this book, *you* are the main character,
and *you* make the choices that
direct the story.

At the end of many chapters, you will face
life-and-death decisions. Turn to the page directed by
your choice, and keep reading.

Some of these decisions may not work out well for
you. But there is a happy ending...somewhere.

In the Freedom Finder series, it is your quest
to find freedom through the choices you make.
If you reach a dead end, turn back to the last choice
you made, and find a way through.

NEVER GIVE UP. GOOD LUCK.

AUTHOR'S NOTE

DEAR READER,

If you had a time machine and could meet anybody in human history, who would it be? Maybe you think of the big names, like Cleopatra, or William Shakespeare. I think it would be just as interesting to meet the ordinary people of those times – like one of the workers who built the pyramids, or who swept the floor at the Globe Theatre. We can only find out about most of these eras of history through writings and artefacts left behind. But the period in which this book is set – the tail end of World War II, and the decade after the war – is still within living memory for some people today, and it's those people who have inspired me to write this book.

It was my own aunty, Rosella Dossi, who told me a family story I'd never heard before about an airman who was shot down over Italy and hidden in nearby caves. Following the scent of a good story, I met distant family members I'd never spoken to before, such as Joe and Dan Quinto, and heard their stories of being among the first Italian migrants who went to Australia after World War II. I also visited parts of Australia I'd never been to, and met the amazing people living there who told me tales from that era as gripping as the best fiction. My deepest thanks to all those who shared their stories with me. You can find their names in the back of this book.

I've always aimed to show history honestly, and this book is no exception. At the time when this story is set, racism was rife. The dangerous theories of Adolf Hitler and the Nazi Party had led, during the war, to the murder of millions of Jewish people, Roma people and people from other minority groups. The world was still reeling from the aftershocks of this atrocity. Yet despite this, racism existed in Australia after the war too, including towards dark-skinned European migrants.

As you read this story, you will encounter racism, such as hearing ignorant characters say that migrants are 'dirty' or 'too thick to learn English', or using the taunt 'wog' – a very racist slur in the 1950s against anyone from Southern Europe or the Middle East. (These days in Australia, the word has been 'reclaimed' – some people who are from Southern

Europe or the Middle East will happily use it to describe themselves, though it's probably best avoided if you aren't from those backgrounds. It is still an offensive, racist word in Britain.) Racism was not okay in the 1950s, and it's not okay now. We have come a long way in fighting it, but we still have a long way to go, and I hope being honest about our history will help us to achieve a better future. On this note, thank you, too, to the wonderful writer, museum curator and Indigenous Literacy Fund Ambassador Dr Jared Thomas for his editorial advice on the Indigenous references in the book.

Another big problem from the 1950s was sexism. Before World War II, women were expected to get married, have children, and be housewives, but during the war they were asked to take on challenging new roles – as mechanics, farmers, spies and more. Once the war ended, society expected them to go back to being 'just' housewives instead. In these sexist times, women were often not considered as capable or clever as men, which was very frustrating for many women – including the character in this story. (Don't worry – in the story, you'll have the chance to prove these beliefs wrong!)

People with mental illnesses or disabilities were also not always treated with the respect and kindness they deserved in the 1950s, which is explored in the story too. My thanks to Amelia Padgett, Josh Santospirito and Alice Downie for their reflections on the mental health scenes, based on their lived experiences.

It's really a gift that we can still learn about World War II and everything that happened after it from the living memories of those who were really there. There's a treasure trove of stories in every family that we don't even need a time machine to access – just some curiosity to ask and listen. From the wonderful people I met while I was writing, I've learnt how having a strong sense of purpose can help you to overcome suffering and find freedom. I've learnt just how powerful a multicultural society can be when we work together. I've made deeper connections with people in my family because I reached out to them and asked to hear their stories. I've learnt how important it is to listen to all the living histories around us, while we still can.

EMILY CONOLAN, 2019

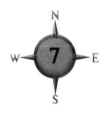

No one leaves their house at night-time. That's one of the Germans' rules. Their soldiers and trucks are everywhere in Lenola. Their uniforms are so grey and crisp that they look like figures snipped out of metal. When they speak, it sounds to you like green wood spitting and cracking on a fire. It makes your skin crawl to watch these soldiers, and you wish they would go away... but they won't. They're here because Italy changed sides in the war, and then the Germans captured the whole country. Now, anyone who fights back is killed.

Mamma says they follow a leader called Hitler, and that he's as bad as the devil. She says the Germans are only good for making rules and shooting people – but that one day the fighting will stop, and the soldiers will leave Lenola, and Papà will come home for good, to share your little stone cottage on the hills overlooking the town again.

You can't imagine the war ending. It's 1943, and the war is half as old as you are – you're eight, and it started when you were only four. The war is older than your sister Giulia, and your brother Tommaso, and baby Alessandro. Maybe it will never stop.

Tonight a summer storm has woken you in the middle of the night, and you want to wake Mamma too so she can sing one of her songs, but you know she's tired from always needing to wake in the night to feed Alessandro. You want to stop thinking about soldiers and the war, so you multiply numbers in your head, which makes you calm and happy.

Suddenly you hear another noise: the growl of a plane's engine. You kneel up in bed and press your face to the small window above your bed. There's a loud boom in the sky, and a burst of orange light. The plane's been hit! It must have been an Allied plane: they're the ones fighting against the Germans. A plume of flame trails through the sky towards the ground. One hit plane means three dead people: a pilot, a navigator and a gunner. You cross yourself like Mamma does when she prays and shut your eyes tight for a moment, trying not to picture the dead Allied soldier you saw last month when you were out on the hillside herding the goats.

Just then, you see something pale and semi-circular, like a second moon in the sky, drifting down towards the earth. It's a parachute, from the plane! It's getting closer!

Your heart starts to pound. *If you ever find a parachute, bring it home*, Mamma told you once. *They're made of silk. I could sew us all new clothes.*

You picture your new dress falling out of the sky; imagine how nice it would feel against your skin, and how envious the other kids would be, dressed in their scratchy old sackcloth clothes. You'll be able to get it, if you're fast. It's going to land just over the next hill.

In a flash, forgetting the Germans' rules, you're tiptoeing out the door. Dawn is close, the sky aflame. You sprint barefoot across the hillside towards the sinking second moon – but there's a silhouette of another kid running in front of you. Someone's trying to beat you to it! You lose sight of the kid, then of the parachute as it falls below the trees, but you keep running.

Soon you hear a moan, low and guttural. You freeze. Usually, if a parachutist lands in enemy territory, they will slash the ropes to free themselves, quickly bury the parachute, then run and hide. But this one must be hurt. Your stomach lurches with fear, and you panic. Being out at night-time is enough to get you killed. Helping an injured Allied soldier is enough to get your whole family shot. You remember the gallows in the town square, where the German soldiers execute any Italians who dare to disobey them.

Then you hear a boy's voice – a voice you know. It's your cousin Mario. 'It's all right, I won't let them get you,' he's saying. 'Where does it hurt the most?'

You tiptoe over the crest of the hill and see a tangle of ropes; a swathe of silk like the skin on hot milk; a crumpled dark figure; and Mario kneeling over him. Mario looks up and sees you standing there.

'Get down here!' he hisses. 'Now!' You scramble over loose rocks, your hand against the hillside for balance, until you arrive, skitter-bump, at Mario's feet.

The parachutist looks pale and sweaty. One leg sticks out at a bad angle, making you feel sick. He's gripping his thigh and, under his hands, a dark stain spreads. He groans through clenched teeth. There is no sign of anyone else from the plane.

'This is bad,' you hiss at Mario.

'I know. Shut up!' he snaps.

'That's blood,' you say, feeling a shiver of fear as you realise that the parachutist's thigh bone must have snapped and pierced his skin.

'I know. I said shut *up*, all right? Let me think!'

You hop from one foot to the other, glancing nervously at the lightening sky. If you stay, you might get caught by a German dawn patrol. They'll be combing the hillside soon enough, looking for the plane they shot down. You want to help this man – and if you're honest, you still want his parachute too – but you don't think you and Mario can save him alone.

'I'm going to get our mammas,' you say, turning for home. Mamma is a midwife, used to the sight of blood, and Zia Rosa is strong as an ox. They can decide if it's worth the risk to carry him home.

'Stop, no!' cries Mario. He grabs your wrist. 'I need you here – I think the two of us can do it together.'

'Do what?'

'Help him to Cat's Mouth.'

The cave Mario's talking about is only a few hundred metres from here, with needle-like rocks all around the rim, which is why it's called Cat's Mouth. The winding tunnels inside are known as the cat's guts.

'No, I'll get our mammas to help,' you insist.

'We can't wait that long!' cries Mario. 'By the time you get back, it'll be dawn. Help me now!'

✴ If you leave to get help from an adult, go to page 12.

✴ If you stay and help Mario, go to page 15.

You break free of Mario's grip and run for home. 'I'll be really quick,' you cry. 'I promise!' Behind you, you hear Mario swear and the parachutist grunt in pain.

Your lungs are burning, but you push past the pain, also ignoring the rocks that bite at your feet. Every time your energy starts to flag, you remember the dark bloodstain and the parachutist's anguish and keep running.

Everyone is just waking as you bang through the door. Mamma stares, astonished, then scrambles up off her bed, baby Alessandro still attached to her breast. 'Where have you been?' she demands.

'An airman,' you gasp, 'was shot down in the night. Mario's with him.'

Mamma turns pale. She hesitates for just a moment, and you know she's thinking of the gallows in the town square too. But when she speaks, her voice is determined. 'Giulia,' she says firmly to your little sister, who's peeking out from under her bedcover, Tommaso snuggled in beside her, 'you mind the other children. I'll get my things.' Mamma hasn't lost a mother or a baby in ten years, apart from the babies born months before their time. You know it was right to fetch her.

But, oh God, now you have to run back. You stumble, and Mamma takes your hand and yanks you along. The sun is rising and the clock is ticking: a troop of German patrol soldiers will have already set out. Finally, you and Mamma reach Mario and the crumpled figure.

The airman is wrapped head-to-toe in his parachute. He looks like a fly swathed in spider's silk.

Why did Mario do that? you wonder, and then you see the blood all over Mario, and the tears running down his face. Your mamma takes him in her arms while you stand mute and exhausted.

'You did everything you could, Mario,' says Mamma soothingly. 'You were so brave.' She turns to look at you. 'And so were you, my tesoro. But the parachutist … he's dead.'

Your knees buckle and you start to cry, your sobs scraping at your throat.

'The Germans will be on their way,' Mamma says. 'We have to go.' She wraps an arm around your shoulders, and Mario stumbles beside you, grim and haggard. You leave the parachutist where he lies. If a patrol finds him, they'll know someone cared enough to wrap him in his shroud. But they'll never know it was Mario.

You finally reach home, safe from the soldiers' patrol. 'One day the war will end,' says Mamma heavily. 'One day, you kids won't have to suffer anymore, and our home will be peaceful and safe again.'

Whether she's right or not, you know that you will never forget the airman who fell from the sky.

THE END

✴ To return to the last choice you made and try again, go to page 11.

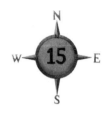

'Okay.' You nod to Mario, swallowing your fear. 'I'll stay. What do I have to do?'

He hands you a knife. 'Cut his parachute off and tear some strips up for bandages. We'll use the rest to carry him, like a hammock.'

You get to work with the knife, noting gratefully that there's still plenty of fabric left for when this is all over – if you survive.

Mario is eleven, and he spends most of his time devising practical jokes, stealing food, and finding ways to drive you crazy. He's tied your shoelaces together in church so you fell on your face when you got up to take communion; he's tricked you into drinking muddy water, which he said was hot chocolate; and he's spoiled plenty of games with your friends by pelting you with pebbles from a secret hiding place. He can run faster, fart louder, and spit further than you. You wish you could beat him, just once.

But here Mario is now, working seriously and carefully. He's like the heroic army doctors you've read about, working in the field to save their men.

He cuts away the clothes around the wound and ties the bandages you've made firmly in place. The parachutist is groaning and saying things in English. You catch him slurring an Italian word – is it 'water'? – before his eyes roll back and his head drops to the ground.

'He fainted!' you tell Mario.

'Oh damn, that's not good. People can die if they lose too much blood. Help me roll him.'

Feeling shaky, you roll the man's heavy, limp body onto the parachute. His arms flop like a doll's.

'Is he already dead?' you whisper.

'No, I can hear him breathing, but we'll *all* be dead if the Germans find us, so hurry up.'

The parachutist is too heavy to lift, so you and Mario have to drag him along the ground. The parachute is slippery in your sweaty palms, and you think, *This is ruining the fabric,* then immediately berate yourself: *Don't be so selfish. Pull harder!*

The fabric is wrapped so tightly around your wrists that your hands go numb. How can one man weigh so much? You struggle to pull until your muscles burn and tired sobs rise in your throat. Cat's Mouth isn't that far away, but your progress is painfully slow. Every so often you startle – was that the stamping boots of an approaching patrol? – but it always turns out to be a falling stone or a bird landing in a tree.

The sun is beginning to warm the stones by the time you reach Cat's Mouth. 'The most dangerous bit is over,' says Mario, hoisting the parachutist's body over the pointy rocks at the entrance. You haul his legs over, and Mario leads the way down a clay bank that is the cat's throat. The light dims to black as you slowly weave on, twisting and turning through the labyrinthine passages. You stumble along, trying not to let the parachutist's back hit any rocks.

Surely he's dead by now, you think grimly. Occasionally you bang your head, or twist your ankle in a pothole full of freezing water, but Mario navigates these tunnels as easily as a bat. It's as if he can see in the dark, but he's probably explored down here so many times he knows it by heart.

After a while, he stops. 'This'll do,' he says. His voice echoes and you can hear a *drip … drip … drip.*

You're in some kind of cavern – you feel all around you for a wall or ceiling, your arms waving like antennae, but you can't connect with anything. Shivers run over your skin as your sweat cools in the frigid air. You've never known blackness like this.

'What are we going to do now?' you ask Mario. 'We can't just leave him here.'

'We won't,' says Mario. 'I'll be back in a few hours with some food.'

'Wait, *what*?' you cry. You hear him leaving the cave and you scream, 'Stop, Mario!' The footsteps pause. 'Don't go ...' you say, feeling like a baby. Your mind is a blur of fears. You don't even know if the parachutist is alive. You just want to be back home, not abandoned here in the cat's guts.

'Well, do *you* know your way out of the cave to go home and get help?' Mario asks. 'One of us has to wait here.'

You try not to cry as his footsteps fade away.

On hands and knees, so you can feel and balance better, you crawl back towards the parachutist. The floor is smooth and cold, mostly clay and puddles, with a few slabs of rock. The parachutist's echoing breaths, and a constant drip, are the only sounds. You bump into his body, and cautiously pat it all over. He's shivering slightly, and you are too. He's not going to survive if you can't keep him warm. Gingerly, you lie on the damp floor, press your body against his, and wrap the parachute around both of you as tightly as you can manage.

Time seems to stretch. Your thoughts become vivid daydreams. *Has Mario been gone an hour yet? Or longer?* You wonder what will become of

the parachutist if he recovers. Mamma says some
of the southern parts of Italy are safe now – but
to get there, he'd have to sneak past thousands of
Germans.

How can you possibly keep him here, though,
without light or warmth? Surely it would send even
the strongest person mad. You don't want to stay
here a minute longer yourself, and it's only been an
hour... or perhaps two?

Suddenly the parachutist's body jerks behind you.
He splutters something in English, and you scramble
to your knees as he swings his arms around wildly.
You catch one of his arms as it knocks against you,
holding it still, and he reaches out to touch your face.

'Hello,' you say to him. 'It's okay.'

'Uh... hello,' he replies in heavily accented Italian.
'My eyes is... disappear? It is black.' He's speaking
slowly, in a voice choked with pain.

'Yes, because we're in a cave,' you tell him. 'It's all
right, the Germans can't find you here. My cousin
Mario will be back soon. Your plane crashed, do
you remember?'

There's silence. Maybe he couldn't understand
that much Italian, but you don't know any English.
He's probably British, or American. Eventually he
croaks, 'You are... a little girl?'

'Not that little,' you tell him. 'I'm eight.'

'Eight,' he says. 'One, two, three, four, five, seven, eight.'

'No.' You laugh. 'Five, *six*, seven, eight.'

'Ah,' he says. 'Sorry, six. I forget you.' His voice is warm. It's a relief not to feel so alone in the cat's guts. He says something in English, as if to himself; then he lets out a long, shaky breath, and you feel so sad for him. He's a long way from home, and even though he's a grown-up man, he must wish he could just go home. His leg must be causing him agony, and he's probably thinking about his missing companions from the plane.

You find his hand and squeeze it. 'I'll be your friend,' you tell him.

'My friend,' he replies, and you can hear the smile in his voice. 'My very good friend, thank you.'

✴ Go to page 21.

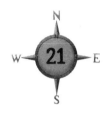

It's been six months since you and Mario found the navigator, Charlie, and hid him in the cat's guts. His thigh bone still has a lump in it, and he's bearded and as skinny as a shipwreck survivor, but you and your family have kept him alive all this time.

'Off to school?' Mamma asks, smiling as she sees you packing food rations, a candle and a pencil into your schoolbag. She sighs and ruffles your hair. 'I'm proud of you, my tesoro – I just wish it wasn't so cold in there.'

'I have the best classroom, and the best teacher, in the world!' you tell her. Although the village school closed at the start of the war, you and Mario have a class of two in the cat's guts – with Charlie as your teacher. Except for an occasional patrol, the Germans rarely come up into these hills, so you can get in and out of the cave without arousing suspicion.

'How does Charlie manage to teach you anything in the dark?' Mamma laughs.

'Oh, Mamma, it's never dark in there, not really!'
you tell her. 'Yesterday Charlie told us all about his
home at Sandford's Rise in Australia, and I could
just feel the warm sun, and see the kangaroos
bouncing by!'

Your English is good enough now that you
understood nearly every word Charlie said. Mario's
is too. You told Giulia, Tommaso and Alessandro
all about Australia as their bedtime story last night,
and they were entranced.

'Just mind a German never follows you there,'
Mamma cautions. 'And if they ever overhear you
speaking English…' She shudders.

'I WISH THE Allies would hurry up and win,'
mutters Mario as you cross the hillside towards Cat's
Mouth. 'If I were older, I'd join the Italian resistance
and – *ker-blam!* – blow them all up. I'd be a hero.'

'Charlie's my hero,' you reply.

'You have to *do* stuff to be a hero,' argues Mario.
'Not just sit around talking and freezing your bum
off. You have to rescue people.'

You know that Charlie has already rescued you:
he's given your mind tools to help make it sharper
and stronger. No woman in your family has ever

studied past the age of twelve, but you know now that you'll be the first. Charlie says so, and he knows nearly everything.

LATER THAT AFTERNOON, when the candle's burnt low in the cat's guts after a long talk about the angles in a triangle (which always add up to one hundred and eighty), Charlie tells you: 'You should think about being an engineer. You got the hang of that very quickly.'

'What do engineers do?' you ask.

'They use science and maths to solve problems,' Charlie says. 'They can invent, design and build great things.'

That's what I want to do, you think immediately. *I like solving problems, and I'm good at science and maths.*

'She's only a girl,' scoffs Mario.

You bristle. 'I'm smarter than you!' you say.

Charlie jabs his finger into Mario's chest. 'Only a girl?' he repeats incredulously. 'Where do you get stupid ideas like that from? Name one thing a man can do that a woman can't.'

'Easy,' says Mario. 'Fly a plane. Or wee standing up.'

'There are women flying warplanes right now,' Charlie tells him, ignoring the second bit, and you tingle with awe and pride. 'British women fly delivery planes. And Russian women are flying light little canvas planes and blasting the Germans' planes to pieces. The Germans hate and fear them so much that they call them Night Witches.'

Mario's jaw has dropped open.

Charlie feels in his pocket and brings out something circular that glows golden in the candlelight. He clicks the lid open to reveal a compass. A tiny green emerald sparkles at the centre, where the needle pivots.

'This was my mother's,' he tells you and Mario. 'See, it's inscribed with the letters "C" and "D" inside the lid: that's for me, Charles, and Desmond, my older brother.' You can just make out a circle engraved inside the compass's lid, with the two letters inside it. You've never seen anything so beautiful.

'Now, Mario,' says Charlie, 'I'm so sure that your little *girl* cousin here can out-think you that I'll give this compass to whoever can tell me first: How can you make ten plus six equal four?'

'But...' Mario puzzles, '...ten plus six is sixteen.'

You have it! 'It's ten plus *minus* six!' you shout.

'Not fair, that was a trick question!' Mario cries.

Charlie smirks. 'Good try, but wrong answer. There's no sneaky negative number. Just ten plus six.'

You both sit there racking your brains for ages, until Mario eventually shrugs and says to you in Italian, 'Poor old Charlie's finally gone bonkers. I'm hungry; let's go home.'

Reluctantly you say goodbye, but at the entrance to Cat's Mouth, it strikes you. You go barrelling back down the tunnels, shouting, 'I know, I know!'

Mario chases you, yelling, 'What? What is it?'

'Ten o'clock plus six hours makes four o'clock,' you say, breathless and triumphant, and Charlie, who'd just blown out the candle, strikes another match. You see his pleased face in the little flare of light. He holds out the compass to you and nods, and you press it to your chest.

'That *was* a trick question,' grumbles Mario.

'No trick,' replies Charlie. 'You just had to think creatively. Like an engineer would do.' And he winks at you.

You walk home slowly, examining the compass. You've never owned anything this precious. You want to give Charlie a present in return, but pretty much everything in your home is practical: pots, firewood, string.

The next morning you remember the little altar above the hearth. Looped around a framed picture of Jesus, with his palms outstretched and his heart showing red through his pale-blue robe, is a necklace. It has a cornetto on it: a small golden good-luck charm in the shape of a bull's horn. Mamma never wears it – it's just there to give the altar some sparkle and make Jesus happy. Well, Jesus would be proud of how well you solved that puzzle yesterday, and you can almost hear him saying, *Go ahead, my child, take it.* So you do. It's not like you to take something without asking Mamma, but she's busy and you want to run to the cave before she asks you to help with yet another job.

'Are you sure?' asks Charlie as you give him the cornetto. 'The compass was just a gift – you don't owe me anything.'

But you want him to have it, because he's your friend and your hero. You skip home with your heart full of gladness. Then you see the German soldiers and you stop, your breath trapped in your throat. You shove the compass deep into your pocket. There are two army vehicles parked by your open front door. Men in uniform are moving back and forth between the cars and the house. The only sound is the crunch of their boots.

Are they here because of Charlie? Should you go inside to try to find Mamma, or run back to warn Charlie?

+ If you go inside to see what's happening, go to page 28.
+ If you run back to warn Charlie, go to page 33.
+ To read a fact file about women in World War II, go to page 258, then return to this page to make your choice.

Your heart hammering, you edge inside the house. There's no sign of Mamma, Giulia, Tommaso or Alessandro, but there are eight soldiers inside. One of them, who has a thick black moustache, directs the other seven. Some are unpacking metal tripods near the window, then mounting long cylinders on top of them. One is unrolling a map so big it covers your dining room table, and another is unfolding camp beds in a row along the back wall, so it seems they're planning to sleep here.

You could be a sparrow for all the notice anyone's taking of you. You want to scream, *What have you done to my family?* Instead you edge back out the doorway.

You find Mamma by the woodpile, holding Giulia and Tommaso close, Alessandro tied to her back, asleep, and you feel a wave of relief. When she sees you, she gathers you in a tight hug. Her face is streaked with tears.

'These men are dangerous,' she says in a low, urgent voice. 'They want to use our house because it has the best views over the valley and Lenola. So, our house is going to be crowded for a while, but' – she pauses and takes a breath, and looks at each of your faces in turn – 'what do I always tell you to do when you see a snake?'

'No touch it,' says Tommaso.

'Leave it alone, because it's dangerous,' chants Giulia solemnly.

'That's right. Leave them alone and you'll be safe. Understand? We'll stay at Zia Rosa's house as much as we can, although it's too small for us to just move in. I don't know how long they'll stay – it could be until the end of the war. If they speak to you, answer politely, but that's all. Okay?'

'And don't mention Charlie,' you add in a fierce whisper.

'That's right, do not say *anything* about Charlie,' Mamma agrees. 'And Rosa and Mario will have to take care of him from now on. I don't want you going back there again. What if someone follows you?'

'But—' you start to protest.

'Tarlie?' says Tommaso.

'No, *no* Charlie,' says Mamma firmly. 'He's not there anymore, Tommaso.'

'Tarlie's gone away?'

'Yes,' Mamma says. 'He's gone home.' There is a fire in her eyes.

The next few weeks are terrible. You wish you could visit Charlie even just once, to explain, but Mamma tasks you with watching the little ones, who mustn't roam around getting in the Germans' way, every minute. It's exhausting and frustrating.

Until the end of the war? you think desperately. That much-promised day seems further away than ever. *And if our house is full of Germans, doesn't that make us a target? If the Allies bomb our house, they'll kill eight Germans. They might not mind if we're killed too.*

Some of the soldiers aren't as bad as others. There's one with a bit of a tummy who smiles at you occasionally, and once he took Alessandro from Mamma's arms and bounced him on his knee while Mamma finished preparing dinner for them all. You could tell from his easy manner that he knew how to hold a baby; maybe he has children of his own at home.

But Mamma suspects one of them of stealing her cornetto, and she's frantic about it. You had no idea she'd notice it was gone, let alone be this upset about it, and you feel so guilty that you can't bring yourself to confess.

When you finally ask, 'Is it really so important, Mamma?' she explodes.

'*Important?* That cornetto is a good-luck charm! It belonged to my great-great-grandfather, Domenico Franco! He was the one who bought this land, and his father gave him the cornetto to bless his home and family. It protects us from the evil eye. If we don't get it back, our luck will go from bad to worse, mark my words.'

The evil eye. You think of it like Satan's eye, jealous and destructive, watching you everywhere you go. You know Mamma must be right, because the moment you took the cornetto away, the Germans moved in. You have to get it back. If only you'd realised sooner that it was so old and powerful.

Mario still visits Charlie each day, so the next time you see him at his place, you give Mario the compass with the emerald and tell him to return it, apologise, and get back Mamma's cornetto. But when Mario returns, his face is stricken. He hands you back the compass and shakes his head. 'He's gone,' he whispers. 'Charlie's not there.'

Your heart sinks. 'Gone? He can't be! Do you think they found him?'

'Well, last week he asked me to bring him a set of my papà's old clothes, so I reckon he was planning his escape.' Mario is whispering, even though there are no German soldiers living in *his* house.

'But he didn't even say goodbye,' you murmur, a huge lump in your throat.

'No note, nothing,' Mario agrees. 'His blanket, firewood – and the cornetto, of course – all vanished, like no one was ever there.'

Oh Charlie, you think, hot tears pricking your eyes. He was your first adult friend, and the only person you've ever met from outside of Lenola. He taught you so much, and he told you that you could be anything you wanted, as good as any boy, or better. Now he's gone – and he's taken all your family's good luck with him.

✦ Go to page 37.

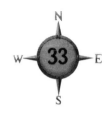

You decide to run back and warn Charlie. If the Germans have heard there's an enemy soldier hidden inside the cat's guts, they'll be coming for Charlie with torches and guns. Maybe you can help him find a really good hiding space: a hole near the ceiling, or a nook you can push a big rock in front of.

You've never run so fast in your life – if you had wings, you'd probably lift off. Your stomach is clenching with fear, and with hatred for the Germans. *I won't let them shoot Charlie. They'll have to shoot me first.*

Cat's Mouth is just over the next hill when you hear a branch break. You whirl around and see a German soldier behind you. Your heart leaps into your mouth.

'Why are you running?' he asks in a heavy accent. His blue eyes regard you sternly. 'I want to know... for why you are running when we come to your house.'

Your hands are trembling and your skin feels clammy. He followed you the whole way here.

'Because of my ... cat,' you lie. 'She's lost. I think she went that way.' You point to a spot out to your right, where there are some steep cliffs on the other side of the trees.

'A cat,' the soldier repeats. 'A lost cat.'

'Here, kitty, kitty, kitty,' you call in a voice that sounds tinny and strained even to yourself.

To your horror, the German walks straight past you and up to the crest of the hill, from where he can clearly see the Cat's Mouth cave. He sniffs the air. 'I smell smoke ... and food,' he says. Tonight, of all nights, Charlie's chosen to light a little fire.

The soldier mutters something in German, draws his rifle and stalks towards the cave. Your mind is in a desperate whirl. *Do something, anything, to distract him.*

'My cat, sir!' you cry, feeling foolish. 'I just saw her over there! Help me catch her!' The soldier doesn't even look at you.

A darker, more awful thought slips into your mind. *Even if I distract him now, he's not going to forget what he saw. He knows something's up, and he'll tell the others. Charlie's dead, and so am I and my whole family ... unless ... both of us together can kill this man.*

Charlie doesn't have a gun, but he has rope and

he's strong, despite his gammy leg. If you can get the German's gun away from him, Charlie will have a better chance of beating him.

You shout at the top of your voice, hoping that Charlie can hear you and take heed: 'A German soldier like you must be very good at catching things, right? We can easily do it – you just have to help!' *There's one German soldier coming to catch you*, is the message you hope Charlie gets from that. *Get ready to help me.*

As the soldier approaches the mouth of the cave, there's no sign of Charlie, or any smoke. 'There's many long cave in here?' he asks, leaning forward to peer inside.

You take a running leap at his back and shove him hard. He slams into a spiky rock, howls and rolls sideways. He's jammed between two of the cat's lower teeth, like a beetle on its back, and he fires, bullets ricocheting off the roof of Cat's Mouth and sharp pieces of rock exploding all around you.

Suddenly you see Charlie charging towards the pinned soldier, armed with a huge rock. The soldier twists his head and takes aim at him.

'No!' you scream. You catapult yourself through the air and land on top of the gun, just as the soldier fires.

A burning-hot shock wave shoots through your body. It leaves room for only one thought: *I've saved Charlie.*

You dimly hear him roar as he hurls himself at the soldier. Vaguely you feel him roll you off the gun and press his hands to your chest.

'Don't die, don't die,' he's begging you, and you wish you could do as he asks, but it's too late. You open your eyes, smile at Charlie for the last time, then close them again. The pain stops.

THE END

✦ To return to the last choice you made and try again, go to page 27.

Seven years later, in 1951, it's as if you dreamt Charlie, the navigator from Australia who lived in the cat's guts for six months – or as if he were a character from a beloved old book. You never heard from him again. After the war ended, you kept hoping he'd show up; walk into your house for a coffee. But Mamma said many fighters just wanted to put the past behind them and forget and besides, if he survived, he'd be back on his side of the world by now.

As for the end of the war, everything was supposed to have been wonderful. Mamma had built it up so much with her promises that you'd expected rainbows every day and feasts every night. You'd thought it would be like those glorious days when Papà was home on leave from the army: he'd spoil you kids like royalty and dance with Mamma. After the war, you'd thought, everyone would be happy, the streams would run with something delicious like limoncello or apple juice, the goats would get fat and Papà would bring home gelato.

But Papà never came home. He was killed just

two weeks before the war ended. Mamma fainted when she heard, splitting her eyebrow on the corner of the table as she fell. Tommaso started having nightmares, and Giulia stopped talking for nearly a month.

It is all your fault. When you took that cornetto of Domenico Franco's, all your luck just drained away. Your mamma's perfect record as a midwife is now ruined: there was a baby born limp who couldn't be revived; another whose shoulder got stuck and who is now severely disabled; then a mother whose womb didn't stop bleeding no matter how many herbs or compresses Mamma tried, who died within hours, leaving behind five older children and a newborn. There were too many to be a coincidence, weren't there?

Then the people of Lenola started looking for misfortune to tie to Mamma. When a baby she'd delivered four years ago, who was now a healthy robust boy, broke his arm falling from a swing, they said it was because Mamma had been his midwife. It was ridiculous, but people started crossing themselves for protection as she passed.

Food has been scarce all over Italy since the war ended, but without Mamma's income, you're relying on a few donations from extended family and whatever you can grow in your garden to have enough to eat. Luck hasn't smiled on you or your family in seven years.

YOU'RE WEEDING THE garden when Mario skids up and drops to his knees beside you. 'We're going to get rich!' he gasps.

You look at him awry. Mario is full of get-rich-quick schemes that usually end up with him getting his face punched.

'There's a high-stakes card-player from Naples visiting Lenola right now,' he hisses. 'Come and play against him: you'll win!'

You roll your eyes. Unlike you, Mario's always had very good luck, and he delights in playing cards. When he first started teaching you to play, he thumped you every time, until you worked out that there were patterns you could follow. You found strategies for deducing exactly which cards had already been played, and which were still in the other players' hands. Steadily, you started winning. At first, Mario was mystified, then outraged. Now he thinks you're a genius.

'Mario, I'd never play against this guy,' you say. 'He's probably a gangster!'

'Then teach me how to do your thing,' he begs. 'I'll share the money with you!'

'If a professional card-player works out that you're counting the cards, he's going to give you two black eyes!' you warn him.

'And two broken arms,' he adds gleefully. 'This isn't just small change with the boys – we could win a fortune!'

You sigh, looking around you. You wouldn't have long to teach him, and the stakes are high, but the house is rundown, the chickens have stopped laying, the children are always hungry. A quarter of the houses in Lenola are bombed-out shells. Your high school professor told you that you were smart enough for university, but you don't even have money for a pair of shoes, let alone a new life in Rome.

Mario waves a deck of cards under your nose. You take them and start to teach him.

THE FOLLOWING NIGHT, a noisy crowd has gathered at the taverna for the game. You're sitting in a corner, hoping no one notices you're there. You've agreed to give Mario some hand signals to help him win; you're not confident he can do it alone. The cards are slapped down. The player from

Naples, Carlos, stretches his wiry neck and surveys Mario with lazy green eyes. Beads of sweat form on Mario's brow.

Each card dealt has a positive or negative value. By adding them up, you can adjust your bet accordingly. Mario makes the right moves.

Good, you think. You remind yourself to breathe, and to stop screwing your face up with tension. *Play it cool.*

The minutes drag by. You're concentrating so hard that you feel you could burn a hole in the cards. Occasionally you flick out a finger at Mario: *Pass. Now take. Play your ace.* He sees the signals from the corner of his eye. Your heart is hammering in your throat.

Carlos is scowling. The other Lenola players except for Mario have all folded easily. The chatter in the taverna stills, and you hear someone whisper, 'How is he doing this?'

You're just about to show Mario two fingers when a stranger roughly bumps into you, spilling his drink all over you. You gasp.

'Oops.' The man sneers through yellow teeth.

You hear Mario thump his table. 'Hey, apologise to her!'

'Mario, *concentrate*!' you hiss.

Carlos is trying to take his turn while Mario's distracted. 'Are you going to draw?' he growls.

'Yes,' says Mario. 'I mean—'

'No!' you shout.

'I mean, no!'

Slowly, green eyes glowing like a tiger's, Carlos looks from Mario to you, then back. 'Then reveal,' he spits.

With a trembling hand, Mario lays his cards out on the table. Carlos hisses with frustration as he lays his out too – the game is over, and Mario has won.

Right now, you're so scared of Carlos, you think it would have been better if you'd lost. Then you see the size of the pile of notes that he shoves towards Mario. Carlos looks at you with slitted eyes. 'Get out of here,' he snaps.

You don't need to be asked twice. Within seconds, you're running through the night in your sweat-soaked dress, Mario by your side, his pockets stuffed full of banknotes, whooping at the stars.

MAMMA HATES GAMBLING – she'd make you donate the profits to the church in a heartbeat, but you know in your own heart that your family needs this break. So you simply tell her that Mario has a new job and wants to pay for you to study in Rome. Mamma's always been proud of your studies, and a full education will allow you to earn a decent wage afterwards, to share with your family.

But instead of leaping up with joy, Mamma freezes. 'But you won't go,' she says at last and resumes stirring the dinner on the stovetop.

'Mamma, what?' you splutter. 'Why not? I know I can—'

'No!' She slams down the wooden spoon. 'It's too far to go by yourself! We need you here. I won't allow it!'

Anger boils inside you. 'Is this about the curse?' you demand. 'You won't let me go to Rome because of that? We need to start making our own luck.'

'There's no escaping it!' Mamma snaps back. 'Since the Germans stole our cornetto, everything's gone from bad to worse.'

You're boiling with frustration. It's time to tell the truth. 'I took the cornetto, Mamma,' you say. 'I gave it to Charlie. It wasn't the Germans – it was me.'

Mamma gasps, a look of pure horror on her face.

'How dare you!' she cries. 'Just think of all those babies who died!'

Now you're feeling really wretched. 'I'll get it back, then!' you cry. 'If that's what it takes to fix this, I'll find Charlie, somehow, and get it for you! But I'm going to university, too!'

'Do what you like,' she hisses. 'The curse is yours to bear.' And she walks away.

THE FOLLOWING MONDAY, something happens that makes you doubt your future: Mario gets a letter all the way from Australia ... from Charlie!

At first you are jubilant – *He survived! He's written to us!* – but your joy fades as you realise he's only written to Mario. There's not a mention of you.

Dear Mario,

I hope that this letter has found you well. It was my great fortune to be rescued by you and hidden. This letter is to invite you on a voyage to Australia, to my farm to work there. If you can come, I'd be delighted to see you and you would be very welcome to share my home and food, such as it is.

Best wishes to one and all,
Charlie Sanders

Mario rescued him? What about you? Charlie
was the one who said you could do anything.
Has he forgotten you completely? First Mamma
steps on your dreams, and now Charlie. You're
so hurt that you don't talk to Mario for weeks,
although it's not his fault. *I should never have
helped him win at cards – then he could never
have afforded the boat ticket*, you fume. Mario
packs his belongings into a thin metal trunk and
locks it, ready to go away forever, and still you
don't speak to him.

You could go with him, you know, whispers a
little voice in your head.

You tell the little voice to shut up. *Charlie
didn't invite me. He only invited Mario*, you think
petulantly. *And he leaves for Sydney tomorrow; it's
too late for me to join him.*

The little voice pipes up in reply: *So what? There'll
always be another boat! Don't let your pride get in
the way of an adventure!*

You squash the thought. When you were younger,
this little voice told you to take the cornetto! Just
look how well that turned out. You tell it: *I don't*

want to hear your crazy ideas anymore. Anyway, my plan is to go to university in Rome.

Isn't it?

✦ To spend the money you won on furthering your education, go to page 47.

✦ To buy a ticket to Australia instead, go to page 57.

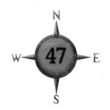

'm glad Mario gets to travel to the other side of the world, you tell yourself, *but I don't want to go. Anyway, I have good options here.*

You know that's a bit of a lie. You would have jumped at the chance to go to Australia if Charlie had offered it, but your pride is too hurt to go without an invitation. And as for having good options here, well, the money from the card game will pay for food, board and books in Rome for a while, at least...

Despite your hurting heart, you agree to go and see Mario off at the docks at Naples, along with his parents. On the bus trip down, Zia Rosa says, 'Wasn't it lucky that Mario saved Charlie's life that day.'

Zio Benedetto, who returned home safely after the war, says, 'I'm lucky to have such a brave son.'

Yeah, what a hero Mario is, you think angrily. *As if Mamma and I did nothing while your family was being so brave.* Mario sits on the edge of his seat, as eager and alert as a parrot, only wanting to fly away.

At the docks, you take Charlie's compass from your purse and look at it one last time. The frostiness you've felt towards Mario is beginning to thaw at the thought that you'll probably never see him again, and suddenly you want things to be right between you.

'Mario, you know I care about you, don't you?' you ask him.

'Of course!' he says and ruffles your hair.

Mario can be a joker, but he's always been there for you when you needed him. Now that he's crossing the world like this, he'll probably never come back. Letters will take weeks to go back and forth; if you're really lucky, one day he'll send you a photo of himself with a wife and baby. You suddenly feel foolish for having wasted your last few weeks together being mad at him. You're afraid you might cry.

'Take this, and give it back to Charlie for me,' you say, pressing the compass into his hand. 'Tell him...tell him I still think of him, and...could you see if he still has our cornetto? It'd mean so much to Mamma.'

Mario looks uncomfortable, but he takes the compass. 'There's something I have to tell you,' he begins, but a blast from the ship's horn cuts him off. Passengers begin streaming up the gangplank, and your zia and zio start crying.

'What is it?' you ask him.

'Never mind – I'll put it in a letter,' he promises.

You wrap one arm around Zia Rosa and the other around Zio Benedetto. Zia Rosa is openly sobbing, and Zio Benedetto's shoulders are just quietly shaking, but you see him dab a hankie to the corner of one eye. Your heart is breaking for them. You know that there's every chance they'll live the rest of their lives without ever seeing their son again.

WHEN YOU GET off the bus back in the heart of Lenola, you smell smoke. You look up and see a plume of it drifting off the hillside.

Oh God, no. Could it be our home? You know in your gut that it is.

You turn to sprint out of town, leaving your zia and zio behind, praying for it to not be true, but someone catches your arm to stop you. It's Father Arnolfi from Lenola's little chapel. 'Don't go up there,' he says. 'There's nothing you can do.'

'But my family!' you cry, the words catching in your throat.

'It's all right, they're safe in here,' he says, gesturing to his chapel, and you feel a flood of relief.

'They're all right?'

'Yes, they all survived, thank the Lord,' he says, leading you inside the chapel. 'But your home … I'm afraid it's burnt to the ground.'

Tears spring to your eyes. You can hardly believe it. Your home … your bed … your clothes … your whole family has nothing left.

Mamma, Giulia, Tommaso and Alessandro are huddled on the pews, wrapped in blankets. Tommaso's head is resting in Giulia's lap, and Mamma is holding Alessandro in an awkward bundle on her knee.

At least we have each other. You run to them and kiss their smoky, tear-stained faces.

'What happened?' you ask.

'It was an accident – the lamp fell onto a pile of laundry,' Tommaso explains. 'I tried to put it out …'

You see that his hands are bandaged and swallow the huge lump in your throat. *Poor Tommaso. Poor everyone.*

Another accident, you think. *Far too many accidents for just one family.* You hope more than ever that Mario can get back your cornetto.

ZIA ROSA AND Zio Benedetto take you in, but there's precious little room in their house, and you know it's no solution. Everyone in Italy has been struggling since the war; your neighbours would have helped once, but now they're as poor as you are.

There's no thought of using the card-game money to go to Rome now – your family needs the money to live on, and unless you can find a way to turn it into more money, it will be gone in a few months. All the children begin looking for work, but there's nothing. By the end of the week, Tommaso gets a job weeding, but it's barely enough to pay for bread. You know Mamma's getting desperate when she suggests that, if you can't find a job, you could join a convent and be ordained as a nun – at least then you'd have food and a place to live.

You and Mamma are hanging out the washing together one morning when you make your announcement. 'Mamma,' you say, 'you're going to need at least one million lira to build a new home, and I'm going to get it for you.'

'That's impossible,' she says, shaking her head.

'No, it isn't – I'm going to follow Mario to Australia. I'll work on Charlie's farm to make the money.'

'As if university in Rome wasn't enough, now you want to leave us and sail across the world?'

she cries. 'You'll never make it! Everything we do is doomed!'

You don't reply. Doomed or not, there's no point arguing about it. You know what has to be done, and you're going to do it.

TWO WEEKS LATER, at the docks in Naples, Mamma hugs you tight and sobs. 'Forgive me for being angry with you,' she says. 'If I can take the curse myself, I will. I'll take all the bad luck for our family.'

You feel like your heart might break. 'Mamma, we'll be all right,' you insist. 'All of us.' And you almost believe it...

She shrugs, her eyes downcast. 'We'll see,' is all she says.

As you kiss your mamma and each of your siblings goodbye, you try and imprint upon your mind the shape of their cheeks, the smell of their hair, the exact shade of their eyes. You want to squeeze them to your chest and never let them go. But then you hear the honk of the ship's horn, and you have to turn and walk away.

YOUR SHIP IS just beginning to heave and plunge as it reaches open water. The land is a distant brown smudge on the horizon. Your whole life was contained in that little patch of land, now getting smaller and smaller until it's gone. How can something so important just vanish so quickly?

You look down at your hands gripping the railing, your new flowery dress whipping in the wind. Mamma sewed it for you from a tablecloth, yet she made it with pride and care. You have no money left after buying your ticket, so everything depends on finding Charlie and Mario, or someone who'll give you a job.

With every rise and fall of the ship your stomach lurches with seasickness, excitement, or both. *This is my life now*, you tell yourself firmly, and you square your shoulders, feeling the wind blow your hair back from your face. *It's mine alone, and I decide what happens to me.*

That night, in the ship's canteen at dinnertime, you find a quiet spot at a table in the corner, take out a pencil, paper and map, and begin to calculate your route, just as Charlie showed you all those years ago. One of the crew told you the speed of the ship earlier, and you worked out the direction the ship is travelling from the position of the sun as it set. You're absorbed in your calculations, and only look up when a shadow falls across your paper.

It's a barrel-chested man with small glittery eyes and bristly white hair. He smells of sweat and cologne. There's a little drip of gravy on the front of his white shirt. 'Hi, honey,' he says in English – but not Charlie's English: this man speaks as though he has a yawn in his mouth that won't quite come out.

Maybe he's American, you think, and you notice his belt buckle, which is gold and shaped like a bull's skull, glinting under the overhang of his belly.

'Let's have a look,' he says, and without asking he jams himself down next to you on the bench seat, so that you have to edge up to the wall to avoid touching him. You're trapped. 'Well, looks to me like you're doing some cal-ker-lations,' he says, rubbing his chin and not even looking at the paper. 'Aren't you the clever one. My name's Bob – Bob Dawe.'

You stay silent. Perhaps he'll think you don't speak English.

'You… speaky…' – he mimes something that

looks to you like a duck's bill quacking – 'Eeng-lish?'

You almost burst out laughing, but just shake your head tersely.

'Hah!' he cries, elbowing you hard so that your pencil skids across the paper. 'You musta understood me to reply, am I right?'

You just want him to go away. 'Okay. I do "speaky English",' you tell him.

His eyes narrow, as if he's not sure whether you've just insulted him. 'Look, miss, d'you want a job or not?'

You're taken aback. 'What job?'

'I've got some business to do on this ship – nothing your cute little brain couldn't handle, just a bit of adding and subtracting.'

You loathe this man, but you think of the one million lira you need to save to send home to Mamma. You have nothing else to do with your time on this trip, and if your 'cute little brain' could earn you some money it might be worth spending time with this bozo.

Just then a blonde girl a few years older than you walks by, carrying her dinner. She points at the man and rolls her eyes, as if to say: *What a loser, right?* You wonder if she might rescue you from this guy if you beckon her over.

'You want the job or not?' the man repeats, leaning closer.

✴ If you say you'll take the job, go to page 62.

✴ If you try to get away from him, go to page 84.

✴ To read a fact file about migration after World War II, go to page 260, then return to this page to make your choice.

You remember Charlie telling you about the Russian Night Witches, on their daring do-or-die missions. If they can do something so wild and glorious then so can you. *Australia, here I come.* It takes you another week to work up the courage to tell anybody your decision, though.

'First university,' wails Mamma when you finally tell her, out in the garden one morning, 'and now the other side of the world! You were always so independent. I should never have let you go to school with all those boys!'

'Mamma, that's ridiculous,' you argue. You know she'd like you to stay, but you also know your independence is not a bad thing, and that it has nothing to do with the boys you went to school with. 'I'll telegram Charlie on the same number Mario used; you know he'll take care of me. This is a great opportunity to see the world, and I'll make money to take care of you. Don't let's argue,' you say, gently taking her hand.

At that, she starts to sob, and you cry too.

You take a deep breath and try to speak normally.

'I'm going to Naples today to see about my ticket. But the boat won't leave for another couple of weeks, all right? I'll be home tonight to spend time with all of you.'

'I'll pray for you,' is all Mamma can manage.

You tell Giulia next, and see a flame you recognise ignite in her eyes at your news. Together, you tell Tommaso and Alessandro, whose eyes widen like saucers. You send them inside to help comfort Mamma, feeling glad you won't be leaving Mamma alone, like Mario's poor parents. But you're more determined than ever to get to Australia.

At Naples, you approach the shipping headquarters and look up the schedule for the sailings this month. There's a tap on your shoulder and you spin around to see a well-dressed man, short and balding, clutching his felt hat in both hands.

'Excuse me, signorina,' he says, 'but I noticed you were looking at these voyages. You aren't thinking of sailing to Australia, by any chance?'

'Perhaps,' you say cautiously, wondering what he wants.

He opens his palm to show two tickets, first class, with exactly the dates you were looking at printed on them. 'My wife has fallen ill and we can't go to Australia as we were hoping,' he stammers.

'Oh dear,' you say, feeling a twinge of sympathy for the man and a flicker of hope that you might be about to get a really good deal. Could it be that your luck is finally changing?

'We were hoping to sell them – not for the full price, of course, but I'm assured they can be transferred to another passenger's name with very little trouble,' he says, nodding towards the bookings office.

'I only need one,' you tell him. 'How much?'

'Would five thousand be too much?' he suggests. Five thousand lira, to go all the way to Australia first class! That's an incredible bargain!

The money changes hands. You thank him profusely, wish his wife a speedy recovery, and hurry to the bookings office to have the ticket put into your name.

But the bookings officer flips the ticket from side to side and snorts. 'Miss, this is a fake,' he tells you bluntly. 'Who sold you this? I hope you didn't pay much.'

The whole world slows down for a few agonising seconds as you process what's just happened. *No. No. No, no, no!* You stumble out of the office, your horror slowly turning to fury. There's not enough of your card-game money left to buy another ticket. You cheated at cards to get the money, and now you've been cheated out of it yourself. *Maybe it was all I deserved*, you think bitterly.

Then you reach into your pocket and your fingers brush something warm, heavy and round. Charlie's golden compass. You smile. It's valuable. *There must be a pawn shop somewhere in Naples*, you think, *or maybe a jeweller will buy it.* It would be so sad to part with it – but what other options do you have?

You are walking down the street when a man steps out of a doorway and grabs your arm, hard. You gasp, and turn to see Carlos the card player. 'Hello there,' he snarls. 'You're a long way from Lenola.' Your heart is hammering. You try to step back from him, but he won't let go. 'I've been thinking about you since our last game,' he says. 'We need to talk.'

You twist out of his grip and run for it, fast as a rabbit, crashing into an outdoor coffee table and hearing the sound of breaking plates and screams behind you. You glance behind you to see Carlos right on your tail.

You see an alleyway, swerve left, and sprint down it, only to realise it's a dead end. Desperately casting about for a doorway, a ladder, a gate, you spy an open second-floor window above you and jump up onto the first-floor windowsill beneath it, hoping you can climb up. Carlos's hands grab your ankles, but you manage to fight him off, kicking him squarely in the face. You hear him roaring and cursing you. You grab hold of the drainpipe with one hand and the top of the windowsill with the other and scrabble upwards. You've nearly reached the second-floor window when, with an awful popping wrench, the drainpipe starts to peel away from the wall. There's nothing left to grab hold of. Your limbs windmill through space before you hit the cobblestones with a *thump*.

THE END

✦ To return to your last choice and try again, go to page 46.

You look away from the blonde girl, back to Mr Dawe. You can't afford to be picky about your first boss, or to turn down money when you're dirt poor. You're wearing something made from a tablecloth, for goodness sake.

'I accept,' you tell him. 'Adding and subtracting are no problem for me.'

'Then you'd better add a little smile and subtract your suitcase from the dorm you're in, 'cos I'm moving you to your own cabin in first class, baby!' he crows.

Oh no, you think. When you first came aboard, you envied the rich passengers in first class. But you'd rather not be neighbours with this man. 'Thank you, but I don't want—' you begin.

The smile vanishes. 'In my country,' he snarls, 'polite people accept others' generosity.'

It's clear he will take back his job offer if you don't agree. 'Uh, okay then, thank you … sir,' you stammer, wondering what else this strange man may demand of you.

Not that it isn't nice up here, you tell yourself

as you carry your battered suitcase down the plush corridors in first class. *If I can work as much as possible and see him as little as possible, I'll come out of this all right.*

That night, you write a letter to Mamma at your new desk, looking out a porthole to the moonlit sea and stars. You decide not to mention that your new boss is a bozo with a mercurial temper; Mamma needs to hear some good news.

Dear Mamma,

You won't believe it, but within a few hours of leaving port, I've landed a secretary's job for a wealthy passenger and *a private cabin in first class!*

I know times have been hard for our family, but I'm starting to feel that I can change our luck for the better. Don't you worry about the future, Mamma, because I'm taking care of it for all of us. I promise that I will send you everything you need and more.

Can't you just imagine the look on Charlie and Mario's faces when I surprise them by showing up in Australia! I will think about it when I'm falling asleep, and of course I think of you, dearest Mamma, and Giulia, Tommaso and Alessandro too.

The next morning, you're woken by a pounding on the door. You open it a crack, and Mr Dawe barges in. 'I need a key for this room,' he huffs, hefting an armload of papers onto your desk.

Uh, no, you don't, you think in alarm, standing there in your nightie with the sheets clutched around you.

'Now, your job for today is to go through these records, calculate the profit, and convert it into pounds. Can you handle that?' You nod. 'Twelve pence to the shilling, twenty shillings to the pound,' he snaps and throws a newspaper page of foreign exchange rates at you. Then he stalks out.

You dress hastily then get straight to it, poring over his books.

There's something very suspicious about this whole business, you muse. *He's trading in something, but he never says what. He seems to be moving huge sums of money in and out of different bank accounts all over the world, but they're all under different names. How can he have access to them all?*

You shrug, and get down to work. You need the money, and so long as he leaves you alone with your calculations, you won't complain.

On the third day, Mr Dawe gives you a long list of food items and quantities. 'Today's job,' he says.

'Halve all the quantities of food on this list, and work out how much they'd sell for based on this list of prices.'

You finish the task quickly and don't question it, until the next week, when he sends you down to the kitchen to pick up a case of red wine from the cook.

By the back door to the kitchen, you see the blonde girl again – the one who rolled her eyes at you that night Mr Dawe first approached you. This time she's shouting and waving a finger at the Russian cook, and you marvel at her nerve.

'Why are we on half rations?' she yells in English. You can spot her German accent straight away and it makes you shudder. You can't help but remember all those months you spent during the war, when German troops had taken over your very home. You can see Mamma's tear-streaked face and hear her words: *The Germans are only good for making rules and shooting people.* You shake yourself out of it and concentrate on what the blonde girl is saying.

'There are three hundred and twenty people in the second class, and we are starving on what you give us – starving! It's not possible we have run out two weeks into the voyage – or if we have, you must admit it, and go to the nearest port for more!'

Half rations? you think, remembering the list of

food items you had to halve and calculate the profit on. You peer past the cook to see what's in the food stores. Rice ... salami ... oats ... tinned fish ... all the items you were halving.

So that's what Dawe's up to, you think. *He's going to keep back half the food that these passengers have already paid for, and sell it in Australia for profit!*

You almost say something to the blonde girl, but decide to keep your mouth shut until you've figured out your next move.

Are they really starving? you think as you climb the stairs to first class without the wine, feeling shaky. *Was this my fault? No, I was just doing what I was told. I didn't know the consequences.*

But now that you *do* know, you realise it gives you an advantage over Mr Dawe. You're pretty sure withholding rations to sell for profit is illegal – and the captain is probably in on it too. Mr Dawe must have thought you were too naïve to figure it out.

Now, you could either take those numbers to the angry blonde girl downstairs and give her some evidence to back up her claims, or ... and you get a little shiver of power as you think this ... you could blackmail Mr Dawe into giving *you* a share of those profits. Less than twenty per cent of that total you calculated would be enough to pay for Mamma's whole house by the time you reached Australia.

You wanted to make your fortune, a quiet voice reminds you. *Why work for crumbs when you could take a slice of the cake?*

What will you do?

✦ To try to persuade Mr Dawe to give you a share of his profits, go to page 68.

✦ To take the books downstairs and expose Mr Dawe's scheme to the blonde girl, go to page 74.

All right, you tell the little voice inside you, *this is where I get a share of the wealth.* You're a bit worried about the passengers in second class – it's horrible that they'll be on half rations – but you don't think anyone will actually starve. In wartime things were so scarce that you got through many days on just hot water and boiled cabbage.

You think about how to approach Mr Dawe. *You're doing something illegal, and if you don't give me a share of the profits, I'll report you.* Being able to say that to this arrogant man is going to feel so good. *Not just a cute brain anymore, am I, Mr Dawe?* you'll say with relish, and the first thing you'll do in Sydney is send home all that money to Mamma. Justice will be served.

IT DOESN'T GO quite like that. The next time Bob Dawe comes into your cabin, you make the speech and watch his face turn red. But instead of throwing up his hands and begging for mercy, he leaps up from his chair, enraged. You have only half a second to realise your mistake before he slams you against the wall, pins your throat with one hand and rips the accounts book away from you with the other.

'Well, well, well,' he spits, his eyes glinting. 'You thought you could bully me? Who're you going to run to, princess? Who're you going to tell about my bad old plan?'

'The police!' you splutter, feeling dizzy. The back of your head is throbbing, and his hand is hot and tight at your throat.

He lets out a scornful laugh. '*De poleece!*' he mimics. 'Look out the window! What do you see?' He pushes your head towards the porthole. 'What's there?'

'Nothing… but waves…' you choke.

'Right, nothing but waves. The nearest land is hundreds of miles away. The captain obeys me. The crew obeys me. And yet… *you* don't obey me. Why is that? The smallest, most penniless mouse on this ship just tried to bite the big cat. You need to be taught a lesson, honey.'

You try to kick him in the shins, but he throws you to the ground and storms out, banging the door closed behind him. You hear a key turn in the lock and realise with horror that he got a key after all. You scramble to try the handle, but it won't budge.

You curl up on the floor and start to cry. '*Charlie!*' you whisper. '*What should I do?*'

Charlie was like a god to you when you were eight years old. Like the old Roman gods, he gave gifts to mortals: he gave you the gift of seeing yourself as something more than just a poor girl from Lenola, and he showed you there was another world out there. But you were greedy and misused the gift. You tried to blackmail Mr Dawe and take a share of the profit even though you knew that profit came from abusing people.

You feel so alone, so stupid. There's nowhere to run, even if you could escape from this room, except over the side of the boat and into the sea. Eventually, darkness falls over the cabin and you crawl into bed, although you can't sleep for fear of Mr Dawe returning.

As the sun rises, Charlie does provide the answer, though, through what he did in the cat's guts all those years ago: in *enemy territory, he hid until the trouble was over.* For you, the trouble will be over when you reach Australia, which is only four weeks away. You just need to escape this room, then find a place to hide or someone to hide you.

Luckily, the brass porthole in your room opens, and you're just small enough to squeeze through.

You drag a chair to the window and pop your head out to find that it's a calm morning outside, without many people around, which will make things easier. The side of the ship is broad and smooth as a whale. There is nothing to hang on to, nowhere to step, but there's a big orange lifeboat strapped to the side of the ship directly beneath your window, about as far below you as the drop from the roof of a house to the ground.

You're not sure what you'll do once you reach the lifeboat. There might be emergency food supplies and drinking water underneath the canvas cover; if stretched, perhaps it could last you the rest of the journey. If not, then you'll have to attract the attention of someone sympathetic on the second-class deck who can either get you out of there or bring you food.

Just then you hear Mr Dawe say, 'Nikolai, this whole corridor is off-limits today, d'you hear me? Tell the guests you're spraying rat poison or something, all right?'

Oh God, oh God, you think, *he doesn't want anyone to hear me scream.* You scramble up, banging your head against the porthole rim. As you put one leg through the window, you hear a key in the lock. *Hurry!* You manage to get your other leg through, and for a split second you pause, sitting on the curved sill. *It's a long way down.* You feel the breeze on your legs and hear the crash of waves against the hull. *God protect me*, you think, and you drop.

In that giddy moment of flight, you are aware of nothing but the rushing of the wind and the beating of your heart. Then you hit the lifeboat's drum-like canvas cover with a bang and feel an awful wrench in your knee. You hear a creak. The lifeboat starts to tip. You scrabble at the smooth canvas as you begin to slide.

Hooking an arm over the edge of the lifeboat, you hang on like a limpet. 'Help!' you shout. 'Please help!'

You know that Mr Dawe might be looking down at you, but right now you don't care – you just don't want to die. Your injured knee is throbbing, your arm muscles are starting to spasm, and your heart is pounding so hard that your breath comes in wobbly jerks.

You look up and see that the pale rope that holds the lifeboat in place is brittle as straw and strained to breaking point. Strand by strand, the rope starts to give way.

'*Help me!*' you scream, so loud that your throat burns and your eyes water. '*Help me!*'

'Oh, that poor girl!' says a voice, and a crowd starts to congregate at the ship's railing below. 'Quick, somebody throw her a—'

Crack. The rope breaks and one end of the lifeboat drops, sending you plunging towards the water. You thrash in space, your screams snatched by the wind. The surface of the ocean is as cold and hard as concrete. As you sink, you're dimly aware of the thrum of the ship's engine, and a building black pressure. Silvery bubbles rise from your nose and mouth like fishes. Then you slip into unconsciousness, and keep sinking.

THE END

✦ To return to your last choice and try again, go to page 67.

No, you tell yourself firmly as you reach the door to your cabin, *I'm not going to take part in stealing food out of people's mouths. As of now, I quit, Mr Bob Dawe. You're a disgusting crook. I'd sooner side with that German girl downstairs than with you.*

'Where's the wine?' says a voice behind you, making you jump. It's him.

'Oh, it's…coming. The cook just had to…get it ready,' you lie.

'What the hell's to get ready about a case of wine?' he mutters. 'Well, make sure it's here by nightfall, princess, 'cos I'm entertaining guests tonight.' He storms away.

Your hands are shaking as you plan your next move. There's nowhere you can go to truly escape from him, and once he finds out you've leaked what he's been up to, who knows what he'll try to do to you. You'll have to plan everything very carefully.

First of all, you tear the incriminating pages out of the accounts book and slip them into the pocket of your cardigan.

Your knees are knocking as you go back downstairs for the wine. When the cook hands it over, you say, 'I told Mr Dawe that girl was shouting at you before, and he thought it was very unfair.' You're pleased to note he puffs himself up righteously, as you'd hoped. 'What's her name and room number? Mr Dawe wants to keep an eye on her.'

'That's Frieda Becker,' he tells you. 'She's a feral little pest. She's in the women's dorm, number two.'

Lugging the wine, you check for Frieda at her dorm, but she's not there. You stash the wine in your cabin and eventually find her on deck, murmuring to a beefy man.

'Hello,' you say warily, tapping her on the shoulder. 'I, uh, have something. To show you. Can we talk?'

'Thanks, Mick,' Frieda says to the passenger. 'I'll see you later.' Mick nods and moves off.

She eyes you suspiciously. 'Aren't you working as Mr Dawe's secretary?' she says.

You swallow your discomfort at Frieda's German accent. *The war's over now*, you remind yourself firmly. *I need to be bigger than my fears – it's time to move on and begin anew.*

'That's why I wanted to talk to you. It's about your rations.'

'What's this?' Frieda asks as you hand her the paper from your pocket.

'It's a list of the ship's food – he was getting me to halve it and work out his profit if he sold the rest in Australia!'

As you explain the sums and the profit, Frieda's mouth drops open. 'The bastard!' she hisses. 'So we haven't run out of food…' She trails off and looks at you, aghast. 'But what about you? We have to get you away from him!'

'I'd love to get away from him,' you say, 'but I don't see how I can. You have to keep this whole thing a secret until we reach Sydney, and I have to keep working for him until then – it's the safest way. When we reach land, we can have him arrested.'

'But people are hungry *now*,' she says urgently. 'Some people who were already weak are starting to get sick – I've been examining them.'

'You're a doctor?' you ask, hugely impressed.

She nods.

You hadn't realised the rations situation was so serious. Frieda leans in close to you. 'It's time for a revolution,' she says. 'I have a plan.'

First of all, Frieda tells you exactly what symptoms to fake, and you spend the rest of the day successfully convincing Mr Dawe that you're coming down with something horrid.

'It could be coxocephalis B,' Frieda tells him earnestly as she examines you in your bed. She made sure she was the first person on the scene, before the ship's doctor could be called for. 'She needs to be quarantined immediately. It's airborne, so I hope you haven't been spending too much time with her.'

Mr Dawe chokes, and runs out of the room waving at his face as if fending off wasps. 'There's no such thing as coxocephalis B,' Frieda confides after he's gone, 'but I've heard it's particularly fatal to big-headed men,' and you both get the giggles.

That night you leave the first-class cabin, supposedly headed for the ship's sick bay, but really you go to the women's dorm in second class. Frieda begins rallying her troops immediately, preparing for a wholesale takeover of the ship. You all meet in one of the empty smoking rooms and lock the door.

'I've tried begging the cook and the captain himself to increase our rations, but they won't budge: they're all in this together,' she says to a circle of angry passengers. Apart from you, there's Mick, a wiry tattooed guy called Sergio, and a very serious-looking bald guy called Dom, who you later find out is an ex-army gunner. They are all Italian. 'We have to capture the ringleaders – the captain and Dawe – and lock them up. Then we can see if the rest of the crew will follow our command.'

'I hope you realise this is mutiny,' Dom says, 'punishable by imprisonment or death. But I'm in.'

Frieda looks around the rest of the circle to see how they're taking this. Sergio has an angry glint in his eye, and Mick cracks his neck from side to side like a boxer about to step into the ring.

'Me too,' they both say.

'And me,' you offer.

Frieda grins at you. 'Actually, your imaginary case of coxocephalis B has given me a great idea. Here's how we're going to do this...'

BY THE NEXT morning, you, Frieda, Dom, Mick and Sergio have recruited thirty-six new 'victims' of the dreaded coxocephalis bug and coached them in how to mimic the symptoms. They form a moaning queue out on deck, and Frieda takes her time examining each and recording their names. The others warn passengers to keep back in case they catch it too, and soon a current of alarm begins to spread around the ship. A nasty contagious disease out at sea with no port in sight could be very bad news for everyone aboard.

The shipboard doctor, who like the rest of the crew is Russian, runs up in a state of great agitation. Frieda takes him aside and speaks quietly to him, pointing to her notes and to the crowd of 'very ill' people. An old man in the queue falls to his knees then faints on the deck; the crowd gasps in horror, but no one runs to help – they're too scared of catching coxocephalis B. The doctor looks perplexed at first, then nods several times and sends a crew member to tell the captain, before melting away into the background himself. She must have filled him in on the plan. You're relieved he's going along with it.

The captain is built like a polar bear and seems just as menacing when he appears on deck. 'What does this mean?' he shouts in English at Frieda.

Frieda doesn't flinch. She calmly explains the illness, then reveals to him that, luckily, she does have a small stash of medicine that works quite well – not as a cure, but as a preventative.

'What I propose,' she tells the captain, 'is that we offer this medicine to the most vulnerable passengers on the ship: children, the elderly, and any pregnant women. They're the ones who would be most likely to die from coxocephalis B.'

'*Die* from it?' the captain splutters. He looks at

the waiting queue of sick passengers and grimaces.

'I bet he'd chuck them overboard right now if he thought he could get away with it,' Sergio whispers in your ear, and you can't help but agree.

'Give me the medicine!' the captain demands. 'I'll decide who gets to take it, not you!'

'With all respect, sir,' argues Frieda, 'that medicine is mine, and I'm not going to just giv—'

'Give it to me *now*!' he roars. 'Where is it?'

Frieda looks downcast. 'I'll bring it to you in your cabin … sir,' she murmurs.

'No!' shouts a man in the watching crowd. 'I need it! I'm feeling sick!'

Other passengers start to shout over each other too.

'I'm taking my children to meet their father – we haven't seen him in six years!'

'Please, I had the flu just last month and I don't have my strength back – I need the medicine more!'

'No, I do!'

Frieda stands on her chair to shout: 'We will create a quarantine zone for the sick, and I advise the rest of you to stay in your rooms and avoid mingling with others. Please stay calm!'

Nobody stays calm. Mothers snatch up their babies and run for their cabins as though they are soldiers under fire. Others press in on Frieda, nearly trampling her, begging for medicine, and Sergio, Mick and Dom have to act as bodyguards.

You, Frieda, Dom, Mick and Sergio return to the smoking room and lock the door.

'The doctor worked out what's going on, but he's on our side,' explains Frieda. 'Everyone else is totally convinced!' She turns to Sergio and hands him a bottle of white pills. 'Take these to the captain,' she says. 'He's built like a lumberjack, so he'll need to take three – actually, four, to be on the safe side – to really knock him out. They'll work in less than half an hour. After the captain's knocked out, tie him up then go and give three more of them to Dawe and do the same. Mick and Dom, you can come with me to the sick bay to help keep the peace in the meantime.'

'What can I do?' you ask her.

'You shouldn't go anywhere; you're too "sick", remember?' Frieda replies.

You know she's right, but you can't help complaining. 'Can't I go along, just to listen? This will be too good to miss!'

Frieda smiles. 'Okay. Just don't let Mr Big-head see you.'

As you sneak along with Sergio to the captain's cabin, you marvel at Frieda's daring and commanding style. *She could lead anyone to victory.*

As you approach the captain's cabin, you hear two men's voices inside and freeze, listening.

'Just what I need, a damned pandemic on the ship,' groans the captain, his English heavy with his Russian accent. 'No way do we share this medicine.'

'Look at it this way, Vlad: sick people eat less, right? So that means even more profit! No one will blame you if there are deaths.' It's the beefy American voice you know only too well.

'Mr Dawe's in there!' you hiss to Sergio. 'You go; I'll wait out here.'

Sergio's English isn't as good as yours, and you have to stifle your giggles as he says something like: 'Tree. You taker tree. But sir, for you is taker four, because you is very fat. He fat too, but more short. Okay, you taker four both. Is okay, four and four. Taker now please. Because the sick is very strong, is bleeeuurrgh, make you dead, like that.'

Sergio emerges triumphant. 'They took them!' he says to you in Italian. 'Four each, the pigs! How was my English?'

'Perfect, Sergio,' you tell him with a grin, 'just perfect.'

BY THAT EVENING, the ship's second-in-command is doing a fine job managing the ship's crew. They all believe that the captain and Mr Dawe are very sick, and are quarantined together in the captain's cabin. Only Mick, Sergio, Dom or Frieda take them their meals – half rations, of course. Sergio did an excellent job of tying them up: his knots are a lot tighter than his English. Meanwhile, the passengers are reassured that the outbreak of coxocephalis B is under control. The only other person who knows the truth is Viktor, the ship's doctor, and he has promised to take the matter to the police and have both the captain and Mr Dawe arrested upon your arrival in Sydney.

That night, you and Frieda are both lying in darkness in your bunks, feeling satisfied and full after a delicious meal.

'You did it,' you whisper to Frieda.

'*We* did it,' she corrects you. 'Together.'

You feel a glow so bright and warm, it could illuminate the whole ship.

◇━◆━━◆━◇

✦ Go to page 102 to continue with the story.

'Help me!' you mouth over Bob Dawe's shoulder to the blonde girl. She winks, and darts over just as Mr Dawe opens his walrus-like mouth to ask for the third time. Skidding theatrically, she manages to upend her bowl of warm mush all over the back of his shirt and he jumps up as if stung.

'What the heck?' he roars, slapping at the dripping ooze and whirling round like a dog trying to catch its own tail. 'You think this is funny, lady?'

Although there's a devilish spark in the blonde girl's eye, her face is perfectly straight as she replies, 'Of course not, sir – I'm terribly sorry.'

The other passengers titter behind their hands, enjoying the spectacle, as he storms out of the room, stopping at the doorway to thrust a hammy finger in your direction and shout: 'And you! You…can forget about being my secretary!'

'Wow, he offered you a job?' asks the blonde girl in accented English, putting her now-empty bowl on the table. 'What a nice guy – you're so lucky.'

You both snort with laughter. 'I didn't spill any soup on you, I hope?'

'I'm fine.' You smile.

'My name's Frieda,' she says, shaking your hand.

'Where are you from?' you ask.

'Köln,' she says. Then, seeing your blank expression, she adds cautiously: 'It's in, uh, Germany.'

She's German? You bristle involuntarily. Those men, who took your house like they owned it; those German snakes Mamma warned you about… *Only good for nothing but making rules and shooting people*, Mamma's voice says in your head.

'Are you okay?' asks Frieda, and you realise your expression must have frozen. Your manners kick in automatically: you hastily try to smile.

'I – I – didn't *like* the war, you know,' Frieda stammers. 'I didn't choose for it to happen – or support what Hitler stood for.'

'O… of course,' you say, realising you sound stilted. You feel suddenly desperate to get out of there. Frieda rises from her seat, and you stumble past her and scurry from the room. You collapse into your bunk, relieved that no one else is in the dorm yet. It's only then you realise you left your map and calculations back on the table.

You feel ashamed and teary. *What's wrong with me?* you berate yourself. *Frieda saved me, and I ran away because – what? – she's German? The war wasn't her fault. She would have suffered too.*

You think how hard it must be for the ex-soldiers on both sides, who had to face the enemy in battle every day; who had to kill them or be killed. Now everyone is supposed to forget the past and share this new land you're headed towards, Australia.

You realise that you've brought more along with you on this journey than just your luggage: your fears have followed you as surely as if they'd been invited.

You're not welcome here, fears, you tell them firmly.

YOU'RE GLAD THAT the boat journey takes six weeks because you need that time to practise English, and to your great delight, there are lessons on the boat! You also need the time to get used to being away from home, and to make friends.

Every morning when you wake up, you remember the smoking ruin of your home, and how much money you'll need to earn to pay for Mamma's new house. You don't regret not taking Mr Dawe's offer, and you often remind yourself: *There will be better things in Australia.*

You have decided that this boat is your cocoon – you came aboard a caterpillar, and will leave it a butterfly. Your first step away from your old self is to make friends with Frieda, who has continued to be just as friendly to you as she was that first night. She claims she thought you ran out of the room that first time you met simply because you felt seasick, not to get away from her, and you love her for it.

'Have you noticed there is less and less food?' she asks you at the end of the first week. You have definitely noticed: there wasn't much to begin with, but now it seems all the passengers are being served half rations. 'It's not enough, is it?'

'Maybe … we've eaten most of it already?' you say uncertainly.

'Impossible,' she replies brusquely. 'We're only one week from Europe; they can't have planned that badly. Surely they have a lot, so why don't they give it to us?'

'Let's look around,' you say. 'We can do a bit of spying.'

You immediately regret your choice of words. *Why did I have to bring the war and spying into it? I'm such an idiot!*

Luckily, Frieda laughs and loves the idea. 'But this time on the same side, for the whole time, all right?' She elbows you in the ribs. She's reminding you that the Italians and Germans actually started the war on the same side, before Italy joined the Allies. It's awkward, but you're relieved she likes your idea.

THE JOINT GERMAN–ITALIAN spying mission gets off to a slow start. Frieda, who is a trained doctor – which impresses you hugely – starts offering free health check-ups for passengers and compiles data on everyone's weight and health. You act as a translator for her Italian patients. People are complaining about the lack of food, and Frieda is worried.

By the end of the second week, a serious case emerges. An Italian couple from Florence have a two-month-old baby who's become sickly and weak.

'I don't think my breastmilk is enough for him,' the mother says, and you translate. 'He's always so tired and irritable. My husband gives me his share of food, but we're so hungry.'

Frieda checks the mother, and finds her dangerously underweight, and her baby not nearly as alert or strong as he should be.

'There may have been a problem before they came on board the boat,' she mutters to you after they've left, 'but I'm worried about that baby. He and the mother need a lot more food.'

Now you're angry. You can't help but think of all those babies back home whom Mamma couldn't save. Well, what if there's something you can *do* this time? What if you can save this one?

The next day, you're on the side deck with Frieda, when you see none other than Mr Bob Dawe, the American, slipping in the back door of the kitchen. You and Frieda peek through the doorway to eavesdrop.

The cook is holding a huge baking dish, filled to the brim with food. As he hands it to Mr Dawe, he mutters: 'They're complaining – the passengers, I mean. They've noticed.'

'Who cares?' snarls Mr Dawe. 'Half rations won't kill them.' He tries to take the dish from the cook, but the cook holds on to it.

'I'm the one who has to answer to them,' he whispers. 'I should be getting a share of the profits.'

'How dare you speak to me like that?' says Mr Dawe. 'I can have you replaced faster than you can blink. Now keep your mouth shut.'

Mr Dawe yanks the dish away from the cook

and storms off and you and Frieda dart away as he heads for the doorway. You exchange excited glances, then follow him. Outside a first-class cabin, Mr Dawe balances the almighty food tray on one arm, fumbles for his keys, and—

'Hey!' he bellows as he catches sight of you. 'Soup Girl and Math Brain! What are you doing in first class? Get out!'

You run helter-skelter through first class, heart pounding and feet skidding, back to the women's dorms where you know you'll be safe.

'Soup Girl!' you gasp, rolling back on your bed.

'Maths Brain!' hoots Frieda, collapsing next to you.

You laugh about your new secret-agent names until your sides ache. 'This is serious, though,' Frieda says eventually. 'That mother and her little baby starve, while he eats like a pig.'

'But he can't be eating *all* the extra food himself,' you say.

'He's keeping rations to sell for a profit,' says Frieda. 'We just have to prove it.'

The next morning, you wake at dawn with a plan. You sneak through the heavy metal doors to the staff shower room, right down in the bowels of the ship. It's a damp jungle that smells like sweaty socks, soap, hot farts and bleach. There are rows of damp wooden benches, farts and mounds of clothes heaped on the benches and hanging from hooks. The sound of gushing showers covers your footsteps.

If anyone comes out now, I'm in huge trouble, you think as your hands move fast as mice, patting the clothes, waiting for that special clink that means – *clink!* – keys, a big bunch of them! You fish the prize out of the pockets of a pair of work pants. Then you dash out of the staff quarters without seeing a soul, up to the light and fresh air of the deck, where you show your treasure to Frieda.

'What will they open?' she asks, open-mouthed.

'Anything, I guess,' you say. 'Maybe even private rooms like ...'

'... Bob Dawe's!' she crows, clapping her hands. 'There might be some evidence hidden inside. But wait, it might be better to try them first on the storeroom. If the keys worked there, we could see how much food there really is.'

'Soup Girl and Maths Brain are on the case,' you say.

Just wait till I tell Mario and Charlie about this.

✦ To go to Mr Dawe's room first, go to page 92.

✦ To go to the food supplies room first, go to page 97.

'I'm thinking Soup Girl and Maths Brain might have some unfinished business with Mr Bob Dawe first.' You grin.

Frieda winks. 'You bet.'

You hide near the stairs to first class, and when you see Mr Dawe stomp out of his cabin, you dash up the stairs and along the corridor.

Clink. Jangle. Clink. You try key after key to open his cabin.

Clunk ... creak.

'I've got it!' you whisper to Frieda.

'Yes!' she cries. 'You go in. I'll be lookout.'

Your heart is rattling like a runaway train as you step into Mr Dawe's cabin. The room reeks of his cologne, plus a meaty fetid odour of unwashed dishes. There's a rumpled bed with a pair of undies on it, and a desk piled high with scattered papers and exercise books. You can't see any stockpiled food, although there's the greasy dish from yesterday, with a chicken bone and some chewed gristle in it.

You concentrate on the books – that's where you

might find evidence. Your eyes fall on a scribbled page of calculations. As you read it, a bubble of excitement mounts in your chest. You run a trembling finger down the page. Here's the evidence you were looking for.

Total cost of food withheld: 6,000
Mark-up of 25%: 8,000
Captain: 3,000
Me: 5,000

He got his calculations wrong, you think scathingly as you read the page. *It's not that hard, Mr Dawe: twenty-five per cent of six thousand is one thousand five hundred, so—*

A piercing whistle makes you jump. It's the alarm call from Frieda! Mr Dawe is on his way! You snatch up the page you're looking at and dash for the door, hearing Frieda's running footsteps and her voice as she desperately tries to distract Mr Dawe: 'Oh! Sorry, sir, I'm lost. Can you tell me the way to—'

You pop your head out of his cabin door, preparing to make a dash for it if he's not looking but – *oh no.* He's only ten metres away, and he's looking right at you.

His eyes latch on to yours. He shoves Frieda against the wall, and you hear her cry out as she crumples. You run towards her, wild with fury.

He catches you in his beefy arms and clamps a hand over your mouth. You bite down hard, he roars in pain, and you taste blood.

'You little rat!' he spits, dragging you into his cabin and flinging you to the floor. He slams the door behind him, and you hear Frieda screaming and pounding on the cabin door. You look around for a weapon and grab the closest thing: the desk chair. You pull it towards you.

'What's going on?' Bob Dawe yells. He kicks the chair out of your grip and puts his boot on your chest, pinning you to the ground. 'I'm not letting you up until you tell me what the hell you're doing in my room!'

'The paper,' you gasp. 'On your desk.'

As he turns to look at it, you wrench his leg sideways and roll out from under it. Dawe loses his balance, and grabs at the heavy metal chair. As he falls, he brings the chair down on the back of your neck.

The crack of pain in your neck sends lightning down your arms and legs, and then they go totally numb. It's as if your body belongs to someone else: you try to move, but nothing responds.

'Let me in!' screams Frieda. To your amazement, Mr Dawe steps back and slowly opens the door. His face has gone pale and he gazes at you in horror.

The world starts to turn black, then bright, then black again. Sound jerks in and out, as though the world were a cracked gramophone record. Everything happens in bursts.

'It was an accident,' says Mr Dawe, and you hear Frieda's cry. 'The chair— The ch— It f—'

The world blinks out.

Then it blinks back in again.

Frieda's hand is on your face. She is sobbing and saying something in German, over and over again.

The world blinks out.

And in.

'Can you feel that?' asks Frieda. 'Can you feel me squeezing your arm?'

You see that she is holding someone's arm: a girl's arm, smooth and light-brown. It takes an eternity to realise it belongs to you.

Her mouth locks over yours and she puffs air into your mouth. You feel it going into your throat, but there's no feeling at all in your chest.

You feel her hand caress your hair.
The world blinks out.

THE END

✦ To return to your last choice and try again, go to page 91.

'Let's go to the storeroom first,' you say to Frieda. 'I think it will help if we can gather evidence before we confront Mr Dawe or the captain.'

At breakfast-time, the staff are in full swing: stirring, serving, washing and stacking in a noisy dance. Breakfast is a meagre bowl of the grey sludge they call 'porridge', which apparently the English think is a good breakfast food. They've obviously never come across espresso and crostata.

You and Frieda step into the kitchen, heading for the metal padlocked door in the back corner. You try to walk confidently, like you're supposed to be here.

A shout from behind makes you jump. 'Hey!' says a burly cook in a Russian accent. He grabs Frieda's arm. 'What are you doing in here?'

Frieda glances at you, signalling with her eyes: *I'll distract him, you go!* But the stolen keys are in Frieda's pocket, and you can't take them without being noticed. You have to get Frieda free.

'I've come for more porridge,' you announce boldly and stride towards the vat.

'Hey, no extras!' shouts the cook, dropping Frieda and running after you.

'There's not enough food on this ship,' you say loudly, and you're pleased to see that your voice carries through the servery and out into the dining room, where many of the passengers turn to look at you. 'I'm hungry!' you say. Then you shout to the dining room in Italian: 'Why do we have to eat this grey sludge every morning? Don't these bozos know how to cook?'

All the Italians, which is most of the passengers, roar with laughter, and the Russian kitchen crew looks angry and flustered.

'Stop!' shouts the cook in English, running towards you. 'Stop, stop, stop! Get out!'

The passengers are now all peering in through the servery. You hope that Frieda is taking advantage of this distraction to unlock the pantry.

'Who else is hungry?' you shout in Italian.

A roar goes up from the crowd: 'Me!'

'Well, you might like to know that this cook here has been giving Mr Bob Dawe from first class enough food for a family of twelve, every day! He stuffs his face like a pig while we're not even allowed a second spoonful of this muck!'

The cook grabs you from behind in a headlock. The crowd boos.

'Stop that! Stop it!' shouts the cook.

Another staff member roars: 'Go back to your seats!'

But a chant builds up in the crowd: 'We want food! We want food!'

You struggle, and the cook holds you tight.

Frieda fights her way through the kitchen fray, struggling to lift up a leg of ham, which is fat and pink as a giant baby.

'Look at this!' she cries in English. 'All the good food was stored in boxes at the back. They are stealing our rations and will re-sell them for a profit in Australia!'

The passengers look confused, muttering among themselves, until a woman with a long dark braid jumps onto a table and translates Frieda's words into Italian. As understanding spreads through the crowd, so does a ripple of outrage. The gate to the kitchen bursts open and passengers swarm in. A couple force the cook to let you go and pin him against the wall, and the rest start looting the storeroom. The scene is turning to mayhem.

'Stop!' booms a voice from the dining room, and you turn to see a giant of a man stepping through the crowd, his captain's jacket barely able to stretch across the breadth of his shoulders.

'We want food!' shouts a voice from the crowd.

Others back him up: 'Yeah! Or we'll take over the ship!'

'First, you will return to your seats,' commands the captain, and as a bubble of dissent rises, he goes on: 'Then I will need ten volunteers to cook an enormous feast.' Hands shoot up in the crowd. 'You are hungry,' says the captain, 'and I know what that is like, because I fought with the Russian army, and we would have been happy to find a worm to eat.'

'Have you been keeping rations from us, to sell later?' you ask him.

'Yes,' the captain says, looking ashamed. 'The American persuaded me I could make money for my daughter to go to school. But I didn't know he would take so much, and when I protested, he threatened to expose me.'

There are rumbles as the passengers translate this among themselves.

'I have done wrong, but now I will make it right. Tonight we will have an Italian feast. You can use whatever you'd like in the kitchen.' The captain smiles. 'From now on, everyone will eat full rations.'

'What about Bob Dawe?' asks Frieda.

The captain's face is stony. 'The police in Australia will be very interested in meeting him. He is a criminal for a long time, I am sure. Some of my staff are guards by his cabin door – he will not escape.'

You and Frieda hug each other as you leave the kitchen, and are encircled by a sea of friendly faces and pats on the back. The mother with the sick baby runs up and kisses you on both cheeks. 'He'll get better now,' she tells you with tears in her eyes. 'Thank you.'

✳ Go to page 102 to continue with the story.

By the time the ship finally docks in Sydney, you are elated. You'll soon be seeing Charlie and Mario again, and you'll be able to send Mamma's cornetto back to her at last. While you know Mamma will be happy to have the cornetto back, you've realised it doesn't mean anything to you anymore. Nothing that happened to your family after the war could have been caused by a missing tiny piece of jewellery. You've left those fears, and that guilt, behind.

You look at Frieda's profile, her hair blown back by the wind. *Luck played no part in what we did*, you think. *We made our choices. We took control.* Together, the two of you were powerful enough to foil a criminal plot. There's no telling what you might conquer next.

Sydney is not the first glimpse you've had of Australia – that came ten days ago in Fremantle, on the western coast of this vast country. From the deck now, you can see a huge metal bridge shaped like an upside-down grin.

A pod of dolphins jumps along in the wake of your ship, shiny-backed and playful.

This is going to be a good country, you tell yourself. *I will be happy here. I will be successful here.*

'You're sure you won't reconsider?' Frieda says. She accepted a contract for a position at Canberra Hospital before she set off on this journey, and she wants you to come to Canberra with her.

'I'm sure. Charlie and Mario will be waiting for me at the docks. At least, I hope they will.'

You tried sending a telegram to Charlie before you left, but you didn't get a reply so you also sent a letter to the address Mario had for him, letting them know you'd arrive at the Sydney docks at noon on 27th November. You assume they received it while you were en route and will be there to meet you.

As you get closer to land, a medicinal tang fills the air. Frieda says it's the smell of eucalyptus leaves – she's used the leaves' oil before to treat colds. You hear many odd bird calls. One sounds like a drunk zia about to fall off her chair, laughing! Another sounds like someone trying to gargle and whistle at the same time and is oddly beautiful.

You join the press of people at the railings scanning the crowd below for faces of their loved ones, but you don't see Charlie or Mario. Your heart deflates just a little.

As the ship thuds against the dock, you gather up your suitcase, then you and Frieda find your way down the gangplank and through the crowd.

'They're not here,' you say, dismayed. *Did they get the wrong time? The wrong day? Did my letter reach them at all?*

You suppose that if they don't show up at all, the only thing for it will be to make your way to the address you have for Charlie's farm, Sandford's Rise, which you guess will mean finding a train out of Sydney. You feel queasy and lost.

'Do you want me to wait with you until they come?' asks Frieda.

'No, it's all right,' you say bravely, although you want to grab her and say: *Don't leave me!* 'You have a train to catch to Canberra, and anyway, weren't you going to go to the police station here first to help report Bob Dawe?'

'Yes,' she says. 'That creep deserves gaol time.'

'Good luck,' you whisper. There's a lump in your throat, as you wonder if you'll ever see her again.

She looks deeply into your eyes and smiles. 'I've never met anyone like you,' she says softly. 'Thank you ... for everything.'

You open your mouth to reply, but no words come. 'Goodbye,' you manage to whisper hoarsely at last, and you watch her walk away. She turns and waves every few metres until eventually she disappears behind a tall sandstone building.

Little by little, the crowd drains from the docks, but there's still no shout from Mario, no warm hand on your back belonging to Charlie.

The biggest noise comes from two young men who are running around the docks like terriers. One has a camera and the other a notepad, and they are getting up in people's faces and startling them.

'Excuse me sir, you've just arrived? Don't you speak English? Hey, why not, are you deaf? Sir!'

'Madam! Why did you come here? What do you say to the locals who don't want you here?'

When they aren't harassing those who've just disembarked from the ship, the young men do on-the-spot interviews with passers-by from Sydney. When they interview a tall man in a hat close by to you, you listen intently.

'Hello, sir, we're from the newspaper *Truth*. Would you care to tell us what you think of all these dark-skinned migrants infesting our city?'

Dark-skinned? Infesting? You are horrified. Nobody warned you that some Australians might not welcome you. You are suddenly scared, as you listen to the man's reply.

'I think they should all get back on the boats and go home to where they came from,' says the man. 'They're dirty – they reek of garlic, and they're too thick to learn English. I think it's a betrayal of the White Australia Policy.'

Your stomach curdles with dread. The *what* policy? This is supposed to be a land of opportunity and hope for new migrants. How could Charlie have spoken of his homeland so fondly if he knew it was so prejudiced? You remember how you very first felt about Frieda, based only on the fact that she is German, and how wrong you turned out to be about her. It is clear that this man in the hat feels superior to every person who's just disembarked from your ship.

Your fear is turning to anger. With your heart pounding as if it wants to jump out of your body, you march up to the reporters. The man they were interviewing takes one look at you and flees.

'What is the White Australia Policy?' you demand.

One of them looks at the other and winks. 'Hello, here's a live one.' He chuckles, and his friend aims his camera at your face and starts clicking.

'So, this one can speak a little English, can it?'

goads the reporter, reaching out as if to pinch your cheek, but you slap his hand away. 'Amazing what they can train monkeys to do these days.'

'Don't touch me, or I'll call the police,' you say, trying to sound tougher than you feel. Clearly these men won't tell you anything, or at least not anything intelligent. You remember Bob Dawe, his hand quacking like a duck's bill – 'You…speaky …Eeng-lish?' – and you want to shout, *I can swear in English too!* and let them have it, but then you imagine what hideous headlines *Truth* newspaper would make out of that: *Crazy Italian Girl Attacks Reporters!*

You turn on your heel and walk towards the train station, thinking, *I just have to find Mario, or Charlie*, but the two journalists follow, taunting you.

'Come on, sweetie, I thought you wanted to talk to us?'

'Hey, I can tell you what the White Australia Policy is – it says that foreign dames like you have to kiss nice white boys like me!'

You whirl around and slap the journalist right across the face with a clean, satisfying crack, only to realise that his mate got a perfect photo of it. He crows with glee, waving his camera, while the guy you slapped curses and rubs his face.

Oh no, you think. You haven't been in the country more than an hour, and now there'll be photos of you hitting a journalist on the front cover of their stupid rag. Is it enough to get you into trouble with the police, or sent home?

You have to get hold of that camera, so you can destroy the negative. But how? You could challenge the journalist to a game of cards, with his camera as the prize – but is that too risky? You remember the gangster card player, Carlos, with a shudder. You don't want things to get nasty if you beat them. Perhaps you should just grab the camera and run instead?

✦ If you grab the camera and run, go to page 109.

✦ If you challenge the journalist to a game of cards, go to page 111.

✦ To read a fact file about the White Australia Policy, turn to page 262, then return to this page to make your choice.

You snatch the camera strap and yank it over the man's neck. He stumbles forward and grabs at your arm, but you're too quick. You clutch the camera to your chest, pick up your suitcase, and run.

'Stop, thief!' yells the reporter, and a dozen heads turn to look at you. Hoping to lose yourself in a crowd, you slip inside the train station. You can't run quickly with the suitcase, so you'll have to try to hide.

You duck down behind a wooden bench on one of the platforms, and your fingers fumble for the little catch on the side of the camera that will pop the back open and destroy the negatives inside. The catch seems to be jammed. You bang the camera against the ground. You can hear the shouts of the two journalists, but they haven't seen you yet. Then you hear the rumble of a train approaching. Impulsively, you hurl the camera over the edge of the platform, onto the tracks.

'My camera!' you hear the cameraman yell, and to your shock, he jumps down onto the tracks. His mate runs towards you, looking murderous, but a shout from the tracks stops him. 'Dave! Help me up – quick!'

The cameraman has retrieved his camera, but is struggling to leap up onto the platform. His face is pale and terrified, and you are seized by guilt. The train is hurtling towards him.

'I've twisted my ankle,' he shouts. 'I can't get up!'

Feeling a cold wave of horror rush through you, you sprint towards him, overtaking Dave, and grab hold of his arm. You pull as hard as you can while he scrabbles beneath you, his face twisted in pain. Dave grabs his other arm and you both heave.

The driver has seen you: the brakes are screeching on the tracks. The buffer of air hits you just before the train does, like a big beast exhaling. You lose your balance, and tumble over the lip of the platform. The train hits you with a *thud* that shakes every bone in your body. You're knocked out cold even before you hit the train tracks.

The front page of *Truth* will now carry a very different story tomorrow to the one you were worried about. You won't be here to see it.

THE END

✦ To return to the last choice you made and try again, go to page 108.

You look at the journalist's face, with the scarlet imprint of your palm across his cheek, and decide that you can beat him.

His mate can't stop laughing. 'Oh Davey-boy, how does that feel? Taken down by a wog girl! Thank you. Thank you so much. This is going to be the story of the week. We'll probably get a promotion.'

'What does "wog" mean?' you ask the photographer frostily. You've never heard this word before, but you have a feeling from the way he said it that he probably hasn't used it as a compliment.

The photographer looks uncomfortable. 'It means... well... um...' he stutters. 'It means a person from *your* country.'

'And which country might that be?' you ask him.

'Well, from... from Europe, I suppose,' he says. 'The *south* of Europe. Or the east. Or perhaps the Mediterranean. Or, uhhh, um, or the Middle East. Just... not from *here*, all right?'

You stare him down until he breaks eye contact. Then you say: 'My cousin and I saved the life of an

Australian navigator in the war. He was wise and kind, and I thought maybe all Australians were like him. I guess I was wrong about your people. Are you wrong about mine?' The photographer's face turns an even deeper shade of red. He looks at the ground, ashamed.

'Davey-boy' sighs. 'Get going, then. Next time we see your face, it will be on the front cover of *Truth*. I wonder what the headline's going to be…?'

'Brave Italian Woman Stands Up to Rude Pest?' you suggest, and Davey-boy chuckles in spite of himself.

'Not what I was thinking, no,' he admits, and as his anger at your having slapped him subsides, you're surprised to notice he's regarding you differently, with something like respect. *This is my moment to strike*, you think.

'Do you play cards? For a bet?' you ask, and they both guffaw incredulously.

'Crikey, I wouldn't mind being slapped around by an Italian wife sometimes if she were as much fun as this one,' jokes the cameraman.

You give him another withering glance, and his face falls again. 'If I win,' you say to him, gesturing at his camera, 'you destroy that negative.'

'Ah, no way, that's my day's work!' he protests.

But Davey-boy says: 'Shut up, Chris. What do we get if you lose?' He raises one eyebrow at you.

'I'll tell you everything that happened on the boat – things nobody's reported on yet. There was a serious crime, led by a dangerous American man you should look into.'

'The boss would be keen on a crime scoop,' says Davey-boy. 'The more scandalous, the better. Chris?'

They exchange glances. 'All right,' says Chris. 'Where will we play?'

Davey-boy leads the way into a place called a 'milk bar' not far from the station, and Chris begins to shuffle a deck of cards he's pulled from his bag while Davey buys some sort of hot, brown drink for everyone. You sniff it, but can't bring yourself to take a sip.

Is this meant to be coffee? you wonder.

For a while, the only sounds are the jaunty tunes playing in the milk bar, and the *slip, slap* of cards. You concentrate until your eyes feel like burning marbles.

That's six...plus a jack...he passed a two, so...

Your hands are slippery with sweat, but you don't give anything away. *I'll show you,* you think, as your concentration narrows to a single beam. *I've got this.*

Your hand gets better...you wait...and, finally, you allow yourself a triumphant grin as you slap your cards down for everyone to see. Chris and Davey-boy moan and howl like baboons. You've won.

You hold out your hand for the camera, and Davey-boy says: 'Be a man, Christopher.' Then you pop open the back of the camera, exposing the film to daylight and ruining all his pictures. Now the slap on Davey-boy's face is just a memory; nothing can be proved.

But you will still give them the story. It's not like you trust their journalistic integrity, but you want to get Bob Dawe into as much trouble as he deserves. You're pleased when they challenge you to one last game of cards before you begin the interview and you thump them again, winning a handful of Australian money from Davey-boy's pocket in the process.

Dusk is settling over the harbour by the time you finish your story, and Davey-boy has a full pad of notes. You've learnt that their newspaper is sensationalist and gossipy, not to mention anti-migrant – *Truth* is probably about as far from the truth as you can get. But Davey-boy and Chris do seem to have a drop or two of decency in them.

They show you to a back street that Chris says is 'full of wog— I mean Italian boarding houses'.

'Stop using that word, or I'm going to come back and beat you at cards again,' you tell them.

'You could never be that lucky!' Davey-boy jokes.

But I used brains, not luck, you think. *I outsmarted you bozos, fair and square.*

YOUR SELF-SATISFIED SMILE fades as you enter the front door of the boarding house you've found. It's too late now to try to travel on to Charlie's farm tonight. The walls are mouldy and flecked with gobs of brown and grey mould. Something scuttles out of sight – *Was that a rat?* – and the whole place smells like sour socks. The floorboards creak beneath you. Gingerly, you knock at a ground-floor door off the entrance hallway, on which is tacked a note in Italian: *For all enquiries, knock here.*

As the door opens, a much better smell wafts out to greet you: someone is cooking a rich sauce with garlic, tomatoes and oregano. It smells like home.

The family who run the boarding house, the Espositos, invite you in.

'There's no room in the boarding house, but why don't you stay with us tonight?' the plump Signora Esposito asks.

'You can sleep on the couch. It's too dark for

you to be knocking at more strangers' doors now,' agrees Senor Esposito, who is wiry and stooped.

You accept gratefully. While you are enjoying your second plate of spaghetti alla napoletana, the Espositos' son, Federico, finally arrives home. His parents embrace him and pile his plate so high he can barely see over it.

You learn that Federico is here on a very brief holiday from his job as a tunnel-driller in the Snowy Mountains.

'They're building a hydro-electric scheme,' he tells you. Splashes of red sauce stand out vividly on his slightly grubby face.

'What's that?'

'It's a way of making electricity. They're damming some rivers up there to make enormous lakes, so they can send the water down pipes to turn a kind of wheel that makes electricity. In a few years, everyone in New South Wales will be getting power from us!'

Federico tells you that his job is tough and dangerous, but the pay isn't bad, and he enjoys the mateship – the workers there come from all around the world. 'You should think about coming up,' he tells you. 'They need women too, as secretaries, childcare workers, cleaners...'

'What about as engineers?' you ask, and everyone at the table hoots as though you've just made a joke. You clench your jaw. You weren't trying to be funny.

'I can't go anyway,' you say curtly. 'I'm trying to find my cousin, Mario. He's working on a farm out near Wollongong, I think.'

'Mario who?' asks Federico, his mouth full. 'I've met a few Marios there.'

'Mario De Luca,' you say, 'but he isn't there, he's—'

'I think I know the one!' cries Federico. 'Tall, funny guy – he'd do anything for a dare.'

That does sound like Mario, you think. *But it's impossible.*

'Are you sure it's Mario De Luca?' you ask. 'He has kind of a big nose, very thick dark hair … and a really daggy moustache?'

'Yeah, could be, could be – I know a Mario De Something, anyway. He's not in my team. But I'm sure it's De Luca. Or was it De Rosa … or De Santis …'

Federico trails off, and you get a sinking feeling. *This is a big country, with thousands of new Italian migrants*, you think. *If Mario's not on Charlie's farm, then I'm totally lost.* You stare at your dinner, feeling uneasy. *But Mario must be on Charlie's farm,* you reassure yourself. *I won't be alone for long.*

'I'm going back on Monday,' says Federico. 'Come back with me and see if it's him, if you'd like – you'll be able to get a job there if you want one. I'll look after you.'

Out of the corner of your eye, you see Federico's parents nudge each other and smile. You bet they're looking for a 'good Italian girl' for their son.

Husbands, marriage, babies, ugh.

'I don't need anyone to look after me,' you tell Federico. 'I'm sure Mario is on Charlie's farm. Charlie wrote and invited him.'

'Yeah, but you know, things don't always turn out as you expect,' says Federico. 'Let me know if you change your mind.'

You lie awake on the couch later that night, wondering: *Is Mario really in the Snowy Mountains? Is that why he wasn't there at the docks to meet me – because he never got my letter? But if so, then where's Charlie? Should I go to Sandford's Rise, as I planned, or should I change my plan and look for Mario in the Snowy Mountains?*

Your whole body feels shivery. There's no one here whose advice you really trust. *What if I'm not as brave as I thought I was?* you ask yourself. *What if I'm not smart enough to work things out for myself?*

You decide that you'll sleep on it tonight, and make your decision in the morning.

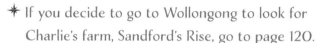

✦ If you decide to go to Wollongong to look for Charlie's farm, Sandford's Rise, go to page 120.

✦ If you decide to go to the Snowy Mountains with Federico, to look for Mario, go to page 123.

By the morning, you've decided to stick with your original plan: you'll go to the address you have for Charlie's farm, Sandford's Rise, and if Mario isn't there then you can try the Snowy Mountains next.

The next train to Wollongong doesn't leave until that afternoon, so after purchasing your ticket, you sit down on your suitcase at the station.

You see a man reading a copy of *Truth*, and when he throws it away you pluck it out of the bin. You gasp when you see the headline: 'Bob Dawe, Yankee Scum Afloat!' Reading the article, you discover that Davey-boy was able to dig up a lot more dirt on Bob Dawe, implicating him in a number of crimes, including money-laundering and high-stakes gambling. It says, in part:

> *This American interloper has also purchased a large number of Aussie properties, including farms, mansions and office blocks. When foreign crooks like these gobble up assets that should be in the hands of true Australians, it's time for the government to intervene!*

You roll your eyes. Even though you agree Bob Dawe is 'scum', it seems *Truth* can't give up on its anti-migrant tone. Just then, a hand lands on the back of your neck, and you nearly jump out of your skin.

'Well, hi there,' says a wiry middle-aged man, smiling crookedly at you. He's wearing a dark-blue suit with a pale-green shirt, and his scant hair is oiled and combed back over his head.

You stand up, your heart hammering.

'It's all right, honey. I just wanted to have a little chat,' he says.

Your skin crawls. Your instinct is to run away from this man, right now. He's looking at you with a hungry, stealthy smile. You grab your suitcase.

'I don't think so,' he says, putting his hand over yours and pushing the suitcase back down to the ground. 'You can't go around giving interviews about powerful men and expect you'll be let off scot-free.'

'But Bob Dawe's in gaol!' you exclaim.

'No, he isn't,' the man hisses. 'At least, not yet. And if he stays out of gaol, the boys and I can too. But there you are, blathering all about it to the boys at *Truth*.' He steps behind you, and something hard jams into your back. 'Feel that, honey? That's my gun. Now pick up your suitcase, we're taking a little walk to that van over there.' He indicates a baby-blue delivery van parked on the road outside the station. 'Come quietly,' he purrs.

You have no intention of going quietly. You thought Bob Dawe was just a greedy fool, but it seems he's a kingpin from some kind of criminal web. This oily man either wants you dead, or permanently scared into silence.

Your heart is pumping, pushing you into action. *Go!* you think and swing your suitcase hard at the man's legs. But with lightning reflexes he sidesteps, and your case swings into thin air.

'Walk faster,' he snarls, pushing the gun harder against your back.

You glance desperately around the train station.

'Not a word,' he hisses, 'or you're dead.'

As you reach the van, you feel a jab in your arm. The oily man is depressing a syringe. Whatever he's injected you with is acting fast: your fingers feel numb, your legs feel wobbly. He shoves you into the back of the van and slams the door. The roar of the engine is a tornado that lifts you up... and away.

THE END

✦ To return to the last choice you made and try again, go to page 119.

'Things don't always turn out as you expect,' Federico told you last night.

You can't be sure the Mario whom Federico knows from the Snowy Mountains is *your* Mario, but you decide you might as well go and find out. After all, your whole life has been a series of weird surprises, ever since Charlie dropped out of the sky when you were eight. Why not follow through on this chance encounter with Federico now, while you have the opportunity? You can always head to Charlie's farm next if this doesn't work out.

You spend the money you won in cards from Davey-boy sending a telegram to Charlie's farm. But several days later, when it's time for Federico to head back to his job, there has still been no reply.

In the meantime, you've discovered you made the right decision in sticking with Federico. The day after you arrived in Sydney, *Truth* published your interview, and as well as reporting on the food-theft crime you'd told Davey-boy about, he'd dug deeper into Bob Dawe's other activities and revealed his criminal prowess extended way beyond that, into other crimes such as money-laundering and high-stakes gambling. A note at the end of the article listed a whole lot of Australian properties Dawe had been buying up with his ill-gotten cash – among them, Charlie's farm, Sandford's Rise!

You can't stop thinking about that now, on the train ride up to Cooma, a town near the edge of the Snowy Mountains. Federico keeps trying to make conversation but you're too distracted, staring out the window. You wonder what Sandford's Rise is like, and what could have made Charlie sell it – and to Bob Dawe, of all people.

Where is Charlie now?

Now visiting Charlie's farm is no longer an option, what will I do if Mario isn't in the Snowy Mountains?

You pass fields of sheep eating dry, yellow grass and patches of what you suppose must be Australian forest: a tangle of silvery-skinned trees and spiky bushes.

The countryside approaching Cooma is mostly timeworn nubs of hills and rolling, fawn-coloured pastures. When you step off the train, clutching your suitcase, the air feels fresh and crisp. But Cooma is in a state of upheaval: the whole town is a building site. Something big is happening here, and everyone has a job to do. Webs of dirt roads branch off the few paved ones. Across from where you stand at the station, a new building is going up, and men are all over the site, pushing wheelbarrows and pouring concrete, climbing scaffolds and consulting clipboards.

Men, men, everywhere! As you walk towards the employment office with Federico, you notice they seem to outnumber women by around twenty to one. A few men pause in their work to stare at you as you pass by.

Meanwhile, Federico is giving you a steady tour-of-the-town commentary: 'Those are the single men's sleeping quarters. That's the mess hall. Over there we take English lessons. The post office is down the road...'

You imagine Mario walking around these streets. You keep thinking you see him, then realising you're wrong.

Why do so many of you guys think a moustache makes you look good? you think wryly.

Federico takes you up some wide steps into a newly built complex and bids you farewell, leaving you to wait in a corridor outside a door marked 'Employment'. He has to leave for a worksite in the mountains, but he's promised to do his best to find Mario along his way. In the meantime, you've agreed you might as well find out if there are any jobs going.

You can smell new linoleum on the floor and hear the rumble of industry outside: sawing, hammering, and calls in many different languages.

I wonder if I could live here, you think. *Everything is so new.*

You think about the wild rivers of the Snowy Mountains, now being harnessed to make traffic lights shine and kettles boil. *This is the modern world*, you think, feeling awed. *This is what humans are capable of when we stop blasting each other to smithereens.*

A call from inside the employment office interrupts your thoughts: 'Next!'

A blond man leaves the office, looking pleased. 'Tank you a lot! I will work hard!' he calls back to the woman standing in the doorway. She beckons you in.

You give your name, age and other details. You even have to step on a set of scales so that the woman – a tidy middle-aged brunette called Mrs Montgomery – can measure your weight, and she whips out a measuring tape and jots down your height as well.

'Let's organise your accommodation first,' she states. She flips through a folder. 'You'll be boarding with…let's see…Edik and Olenka Nowak, a Polish couple. Edik is stationed out at Adaminaby most of the time. That's right up in the mountains. They have two children, Lidia, who's four, and a baby, Teodor. I'm sure Olenka will appreciate your help. Now, as for work, what are your skills?' she asks.

'I've finished senior high school, and my favourite subject is maths,' you tell her.

She raises an eyebrow and makes a note on your file.

You start to feel a little uneasy, but you press on. 'I'd like to be an engineer,' you tell her.

'Can you care for small children?' she asks.

'No!' you say bluntly, and she stiffens.

Suddenly, you feel like you're eight again, being forbidden to return to Charlie's cave, given the task of keeping the small ones occupied. Then you realise you must seem rude.

'I mean, I *can* care for children, of course. It's just that…I don't see how that would help me to become an engi—'

You break off, because someone is looking through the window behind Mrs Montgomery's back, grinning and waving wildly. You scream with delight, and Mrs Montgomery rears back in shock.

'It's Mario!' you cry. 'My cousin,' you add hastily. 'Excuse me!'

You dash outside, feeling like you're running on air. *He's here! He's really here, after all!*

'Mario!' you shout, and slam into him. His wiry arms squeeze you tighter than tight. He spins you around, then pulls back and kisses you on both cheeks.

'What in God's name are you doing here?' he cries. 'This is wonderful!'

'I followed you!' you exclaim. 'The house burnt down, and I thought my only hope was to find you and Charlie, and— Where *is* Charlie? Why aren't you on his farm?'

'Oh,' says Mario, and you sense his happiness deflate a little. He chews his lip. 'Charlie...you didn't get my letter?' He's standing back now, looking guarded. A cold feeling creeps through you.

'What is it, Mario? Is Charlie dead?'

'No – well, he might be – I have got no idea. He...he didn't write that letter, inviting me to Australia. I wrote it.'

'You invited *yourself* to Australia? Why would you *do* that?' you ask incredulously. There's a long, awkward silence. 'Why did you let me believe it?' you ask, your voice rising a notch in panic.

'You weren't meant to come!' he says. 'It was Mamma, she wouldn't have let me go otherwise. I just wanted an adventure...'

While he blathers on, all you hear, tolling over and over like a church bell, are the words: *You weren't meant to come. You weren't meant to come.*

Suddenly, coming to Australia feels like a terrible mistake.

'Damn you!' you explode, and you shove Mario hard in the chest so that he stumbles back. 'I crossed the world because of your lie!'

'I didn't *ask* you to do that!' he hollers, grabbing you by the shoulders and shaking you.

'What am I going to tell Mamma?' you choke. Your heart sinks even further as you realise that you'll never get her back the cornetto as you promised. She'll be so disappointed in you. You start to cry.

Mario's tone softens. 'Look, I'm sorry it worked out this way. But if you just look around, you can find great opportunities here.'

'Don't talk to me about opportunities!' you shout, fury flaring up in you again. Your face is on fire, and you stab at Mario's chest with your finger.

'You've always had all the opportunities, while I get stuck looking after babies! You land on your feet every damn time, Mario De Luca, and you don't even stop to think how hard it might be for me!'

It's certainly not the first time you've screamed at him – all through your childhood, you two were at each other like a pair of cats. But it's the first time he hasn't retaliated. Instead, he simply stares at you, and then he draws something out of his pocket and tosses it at your feet.

It's Charlie's golden compass, the green emerald in its centre glittering in the bright sun. You stoop to get it, and look up to see Mario's retreating back. You want to let your rage out in a good old-fashioned brawl, but Mario is now a grown man, and you're a 'lady', which means you are expected to bottle up your emotions. Now you see why ladies' feelings can ferment like poison inside them.

You put the compass into your pocket. People are staring. You look up at the window and see Mrs Montgomery's face watching in consternation.

I'd better go back in and grovel, you think.

Mrs Montgomery pretends not to have been watching. 'We were talking about child minding,' she says. 'Or perhaps a job in the kitchen – do you like to cook?'

'I love to cook, ma'am,' you lie, feeling wretched.

Do with me what you will, you think. *There's no point in fighting this. I'll just have to get any job they'll offer me, and make the best of it.*

'Oh, excellent,' Mrs Montgomery replies briskly. 'The kitchen is extremely short-staffed, so—'

Just then, a man strides into the room, knocking on the door as he steps through it.

'Betty, I need a tea-lady,' he says to Mrs Montgomery. He is very tall with thick eyebrows, close-cropped dark hair, and a square jaw. 'This one,' he says, pointing at you rudely. 'What is she, Italian?'

You bristle.

'What do you think, is she any good?' he presses.

Mrs Montgomery sizes you up. 'I was going to put her in the kitchen,' she says. The two of them are deciding your future as if you're a chicken. *Is she a good layer? Or will we boil her?*

'Excuse me, do *I* get a choice?' you butt in.

They both look faintly surprised. *Oh, the chicken speaks!*

You introduce yourself and put out your hand.

'I'm Des Ford, chief engineer,' the tall man replies, shaking your hand, looking as amused and baffled as if you really were a trained chicken.

So he's an engineer! you think.

'Sir, I can do more than make tea,' you begin. 'I'm very good at maths, I'm a fast learner, and I really want to be an engin—'

But Mr Ford cuts you off.

'So long as you can carry a tray, and remember "milk, no sugar", they're the only skills I require from you, miss,' he says firmly. To Mrs Montgomery, he says: 'I don't want one who'll get above herself, Betty. Honestly, a monkey could do the job, but it just wouldn't be as easy on the eye.'

Your jaw nearly hits the floor. 'I beg your pardon?' you begin.

Mrs Montgomery holds up one finger. 'If you want a job in an engineer's office, this will be the only one available for quite some time,' she tells you curtly. 'Otherwise, I know the kitchen would be very happy to have you.' She looks at you pointedly. 'There's your choice. And feel grateful you get one at all.'

While Mr Ford and Mrs Montgomery go through some papers, you think through your position.

Some choice, you think bitterly. *Some land of opportunity. Mamma's one million lira could be a long time coming.*

Still, you have to make the best of it, because the

only way out is through. You draw a breath. You're ready to make your choice.

✦ To work in the kitchen, go to page 134.

✦ To work in Mr Ford's office, go to page 147.

✦ To read a fact file about the Snowy Scheme, turn to page 264, then return to this page to make your choice.

✦ To read a fact file about women's rights, turn to page 267, then return to this page to make your choice.

Your time on the boat has taught you all you need to know: it's better to avoid morons than try to work for them.

First Bob Dawe, now this Mr Ford character, you think wryly. *I'm better off getting a job that doesn't tie me to men like them.*

To Mrs Montgomery, you say: 'I'm happy to work in the kitchen, thank you, ma'am.'

Although 'happy' is an exaggeration, you think as Mr Ford huffs out and Mrs Montgomery takes you through some paperwork, explains about the accommodation, and walks you over to the kitchen.

You scan the streets of Cooma, hoping you won't see Mario. Right now, you don't feel like speaking to him ever again. *What an arrogant, self-centred jerk. He lied to his family so he could cross the world with no responsibilities. Now I'm stuck here too.*

AFTER YOUR FIRST week on the job, it's clear that there are going to be pros and cons to working in the Cooma 'mess', as they call the kitchen and dining hall.

The biggest con is the food itself: boiled mutton and boiled cabbage – the smell makes you retch; flaky, overcooked potatoes, covered with handfuls of salt to disguise the total lack of flavour; and green beans that may have once been crisp and springy but are now rubbery and grey.

Why do people cook like this? you ask yourself. *How hard would it be to just make a pot of spaghetti, with some garlic and tomato sauce?*

Pretty hard, as it turns out. Pasta, garlic and olive oil are considered strange, foreign foods here; the head cook tells you that you'd have to make a trip to Sydney or Melbourne to buy them.

The terrible food is probably one reason you never see Mario in the mess – he'd be more likely to shoot a rabbit and slow-cook it with some onions for himself, which you've heard that some of the men here do, rather than eat what's served up.

The head cook is a wiry, tireless Australian called Rich – although he seems to be fairly poor, so the name is confusing. For a man who spends most of his life up to his elbows in food, he never seems to eat. He moves across the kitchen like a cranky lightning bolt, swearing and banging pots.

The other kitchen worker is an older Aboriginal guy called Frank who is unflappable and steady. Although they're an odd couple, they seem to like each other – and they like you.

The pros of working in the mess with Frank and Rich are that they expect you to work just as hard as they do, lifting heavy pots and staying behind late to finish off. They immediately treat you like one of their own, showing you no special favours, but making no insulting remarks either. In the kitchen, you're as good as the work you do – and if you're prepared to work hard, then you're accepted, no questions asked.

So, you work hard – really hard. It's busy, and hot, and noisy, and repetitive, but the company is good, and you sleep deeply every night as the pay steadily mounts up in your account, week after week. Soon you'll have been here for a month and you'll send all you can spare home to Mamma, as you plan to do every month.

You hurry home after work each night to spend time with the Nowak family. Olenka is twenty years old. She married Edik when she was sixteen, just one year older than you. They met in a displaced persons' camp in Germany after the war, and Edik was recruited by the Snowy Mountains Hydro Electric Authority straight out of the camp.

Olenka hasn't seen Poland since she was twelve, and she doesn't know if any of her family survived the war. When you imagine Olenka's past, you see a burnt field. 'No good, no good... war killed all my country,' she says. 'I never go back. I never want remember my past. Is finish.'

Edik is often away on surveying trips, working alone or in small groups, taking measurements for new roads, dams and tunnels. Olenka's life seems to be one of loneliness and toil: washing and drying Teodor's nappies, chopping wood, baking bread, boiling water to wash bedding, mending clothes. Her chores seem to go on and on, like a mountain that grows faster than she can climb it. But although she sometimes seems exhausted, she is incredibly tough. You suppose she's had to be, to survive this far.

Olenka is thankful for your company, your help with the housework and little Lidia and Teodor, and the small amount of board you pay her each week. By night, you teach Olenka all the English you know, chanting: 'You are; I am; he is,' until Teodor wakes close to midnight every night and cries hungrily and she takes him into her bed for the few hours' sleep she will snatch until she begins again at dawn.

THE MESS IS full of workers from all over the globe – Germans, Irish, Finns; too many nationalities to count – and no one here seems to care too much who's from where. 'We're all Snowy people now' is a popular saying. Everyone seems equally determined to throw off their war clothes – the soldier's uniform, the prisoner's rags – and don a hard hat and some sturdy boots and get to work on this great, nation-building enterprise.

But as week follows week, you come to know and recognise the people who traipse in and out for meals, and there are a few in particular who make you wonder about their history. One man, Lauri, always sits alone and never talks to anyone. His face is gaunt and grey, and his eyes seem fixed on a place far away that only he can see or remember. He has a curious habit that makes you think that he must have been very, very hungry once and has never quite recovered. At mealtimes, he takes a full plate of food, walks to the table, and empties it straight onto the tabletop. Then, a moment later, he reappears back in your queue with his empty plate, which you refill. Then he goes back to the table and eats both meals – the one off his plate and the one off the tabletop.

When you first noticed this pattern, you took care

to promise him that there would always be enough food if he came back later. (You'd wanted to give him two plates at the same time, but each worker is only assigned one.) Lauri looked straight through you. Then he went and tipped his food onto the tabletop again.

It seems like sad, crazy, behaviour – but you guess it's not so crazy if you've starved, or had to eat leaves or rats, as you know some people had to do during the war. You know that there's probably no amount of food or guarantee of plenty that will ever take away Lauri's hunger or his fear.

Mr Ford comes to the mess one evening. He pretends not to notice you when you serve him his meal, and maybe he really has forgotten you and has some other girl to bring him tea on a tray. But he notices Lauri.

'What the hell are you doing?' he shouts as Lauri tips his food onto the tabletop. Lauri cowers like a rabbit before a dog. 'That's disgusting!'

Your heart begins to hammer. *Leave him alone, you big bully*, you think.

'Eat off a plate, you swine!' yells Mr Ford. 'We're in Australia now – learn some Australian manners!'

That's it! You burst out of the kitchen and stride over to Mr Ford. 'Why don't *you* learn some manners?' you demand. 'Like being kind to people who've suffered more than you ever have!'

'Don't give me that,' he snarls. Then his eyes narrow. 'Oh, *you're* the one who wanted a job in the kitchen rather than my office. How's that working out for you? Do you enjoy wiping up after slobbering idiots like this one?' He gestures at Lauri who is still frozen, hugging his plate to his chest.

'Much better than working for a slobbering idiot like you,' you retort, and watch his face redden. 'Come on, Lauri,' you say. Lauri lets you lead him to the kitchen, where you refill his plate, and Mr Ford storms out, threatening to have you sacked.

'Thank you,' whispers Lauri before he heads back to his table. They're the only words you've ever heard him say. Frank pats him on the shoulder and smiles as Lauri sits and begins eating his first meal from the tabletop. Then another couple of workers, who witnessed the whole thing, sit down at Lauri's table too, without saying a word, just to keep him company. Lauri never eats alone again.

You're now gladder than ever that you didn't accept the job with Mr Ford. Edik, Olenka's husband, works for him and the two of them have christened him *Pan Spycharka*, which is Polish for 'Mr Bulldozer'.

'Hard man, hard man,' Edik says, shaking his

head. '*Pan Spycharka* doesn't care his workers happy or not – he just say, *Hurry up, you bugger.* Like the boss in labour camp.'

YOU'VE SENT HOME seven months' worth of pay now. A new year has come and gone, summer and autumn have passed, and you work hard to keep warm as the winter deepens, happy to know that at least you are providing for your family.

Mamma's letters to you are full of gratitude and concern. Giulia, Tommaso and Alessandro have enough to eat now, for the first time in years, thanks to the money you're sending. To keep Mamma happy, you tell her you're here with Mario, although you don't mention that you still aren't talking to him, or that he wrote the letter from Charlie himself. You've seen Mario in passing once or twice in the last few months, but you've decided you won't speak to him again unless he apologises to you. You've heard he's a tunneller – the most dangerous, nightmarish and best-paid of all the jobs on the Snowy.

You also don't tell Mamma how freezing it is here. In the mornings, the water is frozen in the pipes, and you've lined your bed with newspapers for extra insulation. One night in the mess you hear the story of a worker whose feet were so cold that he couldn't feel the pedals of his jeep through his boots, so he had to drive home with bare feet, only to discover when he got back that his foot had frozen onto the metal pedal and had to be eased away with warm water.

The snow doesn't get deep and white in Cooma like it does high in the mountains, but drifts of snow form a muddy, icy slurry around town, and the sky starts to darken by four-thirty in the afternoon.

One night, you struggle home from work against a vile wind, sleet blowing in your face, to find Olenka on the floor sobbing. It's nine-thirty at night.

'What's wrong?' you gasp. 'Is it the children?'

'No, it is Edik,' she chokes. 'He didn't come back. He is in danger.'

You know that Olenka was expecting her husband home for dinner that night – you'd all been looking forward to it.

'That's bad luck, but it's probably just the weather,' you soothe. 'He'll be back when the storm dies down.'

'No!' she moans. Her eyes are red and her hands are shaking. 'He will die in the cold. He will die alone ... never come home to us ...'

'Olenka!' you cry and shake her shoulders. 'Why are you saying this? I'm sure he's fine!'

'I just know,' she says. 'I am his wife: I can feel it.'

You look at her tear-stained face, and your stomach sinks. *I just know* – it's something Mamma would have said. She always believed in her intuition. Will you believe in Olenka's?

Olenka begins to keen, and the sound sends shivers through you. 'Edik live in the war!' she sobs quietly. 'Edik live in the labour camp, Nazis didn't kill, bomb didn't kill, but now he will die alone! My babies will forget their father!'

'No, Olenka,' you tell her. 'I'm not going to let that happen.' You don't know what to believe, but you can't stand by and watch your friend suffer like this.

'What you do?' she begs.

You take a deep breath. You know who's responsible for Edik. 'I'm going to find Mr Ford,' you say. 'And I'm going to demand he sends out a search party.'

You march out into the storm and start out across Cooma for Mr Ford's house on the hill. *He'll dismiss me*, you think. *He'll tell me to stop being silly. But I won't go away.* By the time you knock on his door, every nerve in your body is jumping in anticipation of a fight.

But Mr Ford seems concerned to see you there. 'Come in,' he says. 'You'll catch your death out there.'

'That's exactly what Edik Nowak is doing right now!' you say.

'Edik?' he says, puzzled. Then he realises the connection. 'Oh yes, he didn't come back with the other workers – and, of course, you live with Olenka…Please, come inside.'

Your belligerence begins to melt as you stand by Mr Ford's fire.

'It's totally normal for workers not to come back on schedule,' he says. 'I understand Olenka is worried, but sending out a search party now would be unsafe and unnecessary.'

'Exactly where is he?' you ask, and Mr Ford patiently takes out a map of the area and points out where Edik was working.

'Don't even think of going tonight,' he says, as if sensing your thoughts. 'You've just seen for yourself how bad the weather is in Cooma – imagine it on the mountainside. Wait until the morning, and we'll send out a search party.'

You sigh. There's a certain sense to what he's saying. Then you remember the heart-rending sounds of Olenka's wails. 'But Olenka…she's convinced he's going to die out there,' you say.

'Well, she's lived through the war, so of course she expects the worst,' replies Mr Ford. 'And she's his wife, she loves him, so it's natural she's emotional.' Then he walks out of the room and comes back with a single white pill, which he places in your palm. 'Here you go,' he says. 'It's one of my sleeping pills. Olenka just needs to rest now – getting hysterical won't do anyone any good.'

You look at the pill. 'She won't want to be drugged,' you say uncertainly.

'Look, of course she doesn't have to take it,' he replies, 'but if I were you, I think the kindest thing to do would be to pop it in her tea, give it a good stir, and let her rest really well tonight. She won't taste it in the tea if you add some milk and sugar. Take the children from her in the morning so she can sleep in. We'll have Edik back before lunchtime tomorrow. Coming home a day or two late is really nothing to worry about. Happens all the time.'

'All right,' you say, putting the pill in your pocket.

You don't really want to go back out there into the storm, even just to walk home, let alone to search the mountains for Edik. You're just drying off, and it's surprisingly pleasant here in Mr Ford's lounge room. *Was I wrong about him?* you wonder. *He was such a bully to Lauri – but he does seem to want the best for Olenka and Edik.*

As you step out the door, the storm's violence seems to have increased to an eleven out of ten.

'Are you sure you'll be all right walking home?' asks Mr Ford. You nod. 'About the pill,' he says, 'I take one most nights. It's a very mild sedative – it can't hurt her. It's the right thing to do.'

As you walk, you fiddle with the pill in your pocket. *Poor Edik, out in this weather. I guess he has all his camping gear – but what if he's injured and can't reach it? Is it really 'hysterical' of Olenka to think he might die out there tonight?*

You pause at the crossroads in the middle of town. You care about Edik, of course, but above all, you really have grown to love tough, brave Olenka and her two children. Should you fight your way out into the storm, trying to save Edik's life but risking your own? Or should you stay with Olenka, reassure her, and use Mr Ford's little white pill to make sure she gets a good night's sleep?

⬥━◉━◇━━◇━◉━⬥

✦ If you try to rescue Edik now, go to page 155.

✦ If you stay with Olenka until the morning, go to page 165.

You decide that an opportunity to spend time in an engineer's office is too good to pass up. The office is on the second floor of a brand-new building that still has the gluey smell of freshly laid carpet. There are big, boxy windows with a view over the little town, and the room is filled with the scratching of pencils and the clack of typewriters. The men who work here (and you're dispirited to notice that, yes, they are all men) speak German, English and French. They talk about vectors and displacement and cubic tonnes.

Every day, as you walk through the big double doors at the main entrance downstairs, you make believe that you are one of the engineers who work here; that the whole enterprise of the Snowy Mountains Hydro Electric Authority depends on you getting your calculations right. You walk into the office with your head held high, but by morning-tea-time you are always scurrying around like a mouse. You have memorised how everyone likes their tea, but no one seems particularly appreciative.

Sometimes, like today, you linger a while by the

engineers' tables. 'If we make the gradient a little steeper, we can probably avoid tunnelling through that bedrock, but the mining carts might not be able to get enough traction,' says Mr Klein (no milk, two sugars) to Mr Ford (milk, no sugar). You make a mental note to look up *gradient*, *bedrock* and *traction* in your English dictionary that night.

When you get home, you help Olenka with the chores. While she cooks a large pot of soup, you change baby Teodor's nappy, leave him bare-bummed to try to cure his nappy rash, and put the stinky square of cloth in a bucket to soak. Little Lidia comes outside to watch you split the kindling for the fire and sings you some songs she's learnt in English. 'What's *howeye wunda whatchoo are* mean?' she asks, and you try to explain. When you come back inside, Teodor has peed on the floor, Olenka is on her hands and knees cleaning it, and the pot in the kitchen is boiling over. It takes both of you to manage this household, and you honestly wonder why any woman would sign up for this life of servitude.

Before bedtime, you and Olenka sit down to study together. You look up *gradient, bedrock* and *traction*, and Olenka works on memorising irregular verbs, of which English has an unfair amount.

'Why they cannot say *runned, swimmed* and *writed*?' she complains.

You roll your eyes. 'They like making life hard for us,' you tell her. That reminds you to ask Olenka something. 'Olenka … is this what you wanted for your life? When you were a little girl, did you imagine yourself doing so much housework, from sunrise to sunset? Or did you imagine something … special … for your future?'

'I imagine myself dead,' she says bluntly, and you look at her in shock.

'Why?'

'Because for person in Poland like me … there is no future. Every day we are only trying to live one more day, one more day. For everyone, death comes. Very quick death, like my brothers shoot with gun, you are lucky. Slow death, like my father in labour camp, is unlucky. I hope only for quick death. That is special future for me when I was young. Now, my family is start from zero.'

In some ways, you know what that feels like, to start from zero – but Olenka has lost much more than you. For someone who only dreamt of a quick death when she was your age, she has come a long way.

'I am happy here,' she tells you. 'When I meeted –

met – Edik in displaced persons' camp after war, we was sick, starving. Our legs and arms is like sticks. We never finish school. Now, our children is fat and smart. Lidia and Teodor will dream they special future. They grow up Australian.'

You give Olenka a hug. You still don't want to be a housewife yourself, but now you understand that her tireless efforts to make a new life here are every bit as impressive as Mr Ford's dams and bulldozers.

Olenka and Edik's pet name for Mr Ford is *Pan Spycharka*, Polish for 'Mr Bulldozer', and it suits him. The weeks turn into months, and one day Olenka is bedridden with the flu but insists that she can look after Teodor for the day if you can take care of Lidia.

'Come on,' you tell Lidia. 'We're going to *Pan Spycharka*'s office today!' You're about to say, *You can help me serve the tea*, when you realise that you want her to dream much bigger than that. Instead, you give her a pile of graph paper when you arrive, and tell her, 'You have a very important job to do today, Lidia. All these engineers need to know what the new power station that's going to make the electricity will look like. Can you draw that?'

The little curly-haired girl puffs up with pride.

'Does it got to be a very big building to make 'lectrickity?' she asks.

'Yes, huge,' you tell her. 'Can you draw it?' She nods importantly and sets to work.

You go into the kitchenette and cut the sandwiches for morning tea and boil the urn. When you come back, you see that Lidia has taken a roll of tape and joined all the graph paper together to make a sheet about one metre square, on which she is drawing a mighty power station.

'I want to show *Pan Spycharka*,' she says, still drawing.

'Remember, his name is Mr Ford,' you tell her, chuckling on the inside. 'If you do a really good job, we'll show him when you've finished.'

After morning tea, Lidia's grand vision is complete. 'There's the water goin' in, and turnin' the big wheel,' she tells you in her funny little Australian accent, 'and the 'lectrickity goin' out!'

'That's pretty much how a hydro power station works, Lidia. Good job!' you say, impressed.

You don't want her to interrupt Mr Ford while he's working, so you wait until he's on his lunch break. When Lidia shows him her drawing, she makes sure to point out all the people in her power station. 'That's Daddy. He has his work helmet on,' she explains. 'And that's me – I'm the boss.'

Mr Ford barely glances at the page. 'Mmm,' he says.

'I *said*, I'm the *boss*,' Lidia says, pulling at his sleeve. Then, to you: 'Why doesn't he listen?'

'Good question, Lidia,' you say, barely keeping a lid on your frustration. Does he think he's so important he can't take two minutes to notice someone smaller than himself? 'Why *don't* you listen, Mr Ford?'

'Because it's utter nonsense, that's why,' he snaps, and you see Lidia's face fall. 'She'll no more be the boss of a power station than I'll be the first man on the moon! Go back to drawing ponies and princesses,' he harrumphs.

Tears well up in Lidia's eyes. You want to throttle him. *What is his problem?*

'Why are you so cruel?' you ask, unable to catch the words before they fly out of your mouth. 'Does it make you feel big to put other people down?'

Mr Ford rises from his chair and towers over you. 'Milk, no sugar,' he growls. 'This system works because everyone stays in their place. If you cross me again, I'll see to it that you can't find work anywhere in New South Wales. Now take the child home.'

'Her mother's sick—'

'*I'm* sick of *your* attitude,' he growls. 'This is no place for a little girl, and it never will be. Get out of my sight.'

Lidia sobs so much that you have to carry her all the way home. 'He had no reason to be mean to you like that,' you tell her. 'He's just a grumpy old stinky fart.' She giggles in between her tears.

The next morning you get to the office half an hour earlier than everyone else and glue Lidia's picture firmly to a wall. Every time you see it, it inspires you to prove Mr Ford wrong.

You still eavesdrop on the engineers' conversations, and you have started emptying their wastepaper baskets so that you can pore over their calculations before you throw them away. You're learning a lot about how engineers think, how they solve problems, and how they triple-check their solutions using different methods. This will be the biggest hydro-electric power scheme in the Southern Hemisphere, and the project has already broken the tunnelling speed world record. You imagine the joy of flicking an electric switch to heat your room, turn on a light, or listen to music, and the satisfaction of knowing that you helped make that power. You're just waiting for your moment to prove to everyone in this office that you understand what they are doing, and that you are ready to learn more.

Seven months into your time at Cooma, when winter has well and truly set in, Mr Ford tells you that the whole office will be empty the next day and that you can take the day off. 'The boys and I will be out on a grand tour, inspecting all the tunnels to check they're on course,' he explains.

This is my chance! you think. *I can spend a whole day in the office while no one's here. I can read all their charts, and go over all their calculations, to see if I can learn from them!* Then, on second thoughts, you wonder if Mr Ford might actually let you come on the tunnel inspection. *I've never been underground and seen the scheme in operation*, you reason. *I'd actually be able to see the project in real life, not just in theory. Maybe I'd learn more from that.*

⬥━◈━━◇━━━◇━━◈━⬥

✦ To ask Mr Ford to take you on the tunnel inspection, go to page 168.

✦ To stay in the office and check the calculations, go to page 173.

You take the pill out of your pocket and throw it away, where it lands in an icy puddle.

Go to hell, Mr Ford, you think. *You wanted me to dope my friend without her consent and leave her husband out there to die in this storm. I'm made of tougher stuff than that.*

You think about the map you saw in Mr Ford's house. There was a road that would take you close to the right area by car, although you'd still then have to walk more than five kilometres off the road. The most direct route would be to forget driving and cut straight across country. No car could manage the road in this state anyway, you decide – it would be too icy. Cross-country it is.

You get home and pack food and blankets. Luckily Olenka has a map that's nearly as good as Mr Ford's, so you take that too. You stash a heavy metal torch in the pocket of your oilskin jacket, put on an extra-bulky pair of woollen socks under your boots, and you're ready. *I already have a compass*, you think, rubbing the gold disc in your pocket for good luck. *Help me out there, Charlie.*

You tell Olenka that Mr Ford has agreed to send out a search party (which he has, but not until tomorrow). You don't want her to know you're heading off alone. She kisses you on both cheeks and you tell her to get some sleep, if she can.

You walk past the men's sleeping quarters, where a curious face at the window watches you go by, and towards the outskirts of town. The wind is still howling and the trees are tossing wildly in the wind, making a sound like crashing waves. You take one last look at the streets and lights of Cooma. You take out your map, work out your direction, and head into the bush.

The snow is still patchy here, but you guess it will get thicker. *What are you doing?* Mamma says in your head. *You're asking for trouble – you'll never escape the curse!* You press on, the yellow orb of torchlight bobbing in front of you. You stop to consult the compass every so often.

Look at me, Mamma. I'm doing this. No curse can tell me what I can and can't do!

You hear a crashing in the bushes behind you. 'Who's there?' you shout. The hairs on the back of your neck stand on end.

Is it an animal? You pick up a rock to arm yourself. When a shadowy figure lurches from the bushes, you nearly smash it with the rock, before you realise it's—

'Mario!' you cry, your heart pounding with relief.

'My mate saw you through the window and guessed you were going after Edik,' he explains. 'But you can't go on a midnight rescue mission without me. That's the rule.'

Despite the horrible storm, you feel a warm glow inside that has been missing ever since you quarrelled. You throw your arms around him. 'I'm sorry,' you mumble into his coat. 'I missed you.'

'Hey,' he says, drawing back and squeezing your shoulders, 'I was the idiot... I always have been. The only mistake you made was thinking that Charlie would write a letter to me and forget about you. You were his favourite by a mile!'

You laugh. 'Poor Charlie. I wonder what happened to him.' Then a fresh lash of sleet brings your attention back to Edik. 'Come on,' you say.

For the next four or five hours, you and Mario push on steadily through the night, cursing the weather and checking your compass and map repeatedly to make sure you're on track. It didn't look as far on the map, and your progress through the dense bush is tortuous, every step a fight against the branches that whip and snag you viciously.

You stop for a breather. Despite the freezing cold, your heart is pounding and you've built up a sweat under your heavy clothes.

Then you hear it. 'Helllooo?' It's a call so faint you might have imagined it, over the hill to your right.

'Edik?' Mario shouts.

You push on in the direction of the sound. The rain has stopped, but the wind is still icy. You have to hurry – you're close now, you're sure of it!

'Help!' comes the voice, distinct now and much closer.

'Edik!' you shout.

Mario grabs your hand and you smash through those last few metres of bush together.

'There he is!' you cry. Then, as you close the gap between you and Edik in a sprint, you realise with horror that Olenka was right to be so afraid – Edik has been crushed by a fallen tree. He's lying in the mud, wet and shaking. The trunk across both his legs is wide as a table.

You shudder. *Will there be anything left of his legs under there?*

'Oh, thank God, thank God!' Edik mumbles. You drop to your knees and scoop up his shoulders and head. He's a strong man, but right now he can barely lift his arms to embrace you. You wipe the sodden hair from his face.

'It's okay,' you promise, 'we'll get you out of here.'

He looks around and sees Mario. 'Are there others to help?' he asks weakly.

'No, just us,' you say.

Fear ghosts across Edik's face. 'But … it's a bloody big tree,' he says, using the Australian swearword perfectly.

You half-grimace, half-smile. 'Well, I'm a bloody strong woman,' you counter, 'so it's met its match.'

You wish you felt as brave as you're trying to sound.

You force yourself to take a closer look at the place where Edik's thighs disappear under the enormous trunk. The bark is grey and smooth as stone. Edik's work pants are blackened and mottled, but you can't tell if it's by dirt or blood. *Why didn't I bring an axe, or a saw?* you curse yourself. *Or even a shovel!*

You run around the tree and find Edik's feet poking out the other side, wedged against the ground at a horrible angle.

'Edik, tell me if you can feel anything,' you say, kneeling to remove his boots with shaking hands. His feet are grey as mashed newspaper, with swirls of vivid purple. 'Can you feel that?' you say, wiggling his toes, sickeningly sure that he can't. His flesh is lifeless and cold to the touch.

'He's shaking his head,' replies Mario heavily. He comes to join you on your side of the tree. 'Edik's gear is just over there,' he mutters. 'His radio's broken, but he has a shovel, so we can try to dig him out, but…even if we can get him out, I don't know if…'

'Don't say it,' you hiss. You know Edik's injuries are terrible, but you can't bear to think about it. In your mind's eye, you see Olenka, Lidia and little Teodor. Edik's family. *Whether or not he can ever walk again, they love him and they want him home. We just have to get him out alive.*

You make Edik as comfortable as you can with the blankets. Edik's eyes close and he lets out a shaky sigh.

The digging is hard going, the ground lumpy with rocks and tree roots, but you don't let yourself slow down, even though you're exhausted.. After what seems like hours, the sky lightens and birds begin their cackling chorus. You and Mario are halfway under the tree by now. Steam rises off your sodden backs as the sun strikes them. The storm has blown itself out.

After another two hours of digging, you have finally completed your trench under the tree. Edik's legs now lie beside a pit of loose dirt and stones, with just enough room to drag him out from under the trunk. He couldn't feel it when you dug around his lower legs, and mercifully stayed asleep until just before dawn. For the last two hours, you've been digging around his thighs, which is where he still has some feeling, and as the pressure comes off them, he starts to groan and then screams in agony.

You're aware that the weight of the tree may have stopped the worst of the bleeding. Mario has ripped up his shirt to make tourniquets. While you tie them tightly around each thigh, Mario makes a stretcher with two strong branches and your raincoats.

You pause and glance at your hands. They're burning, raw with scrapes and blisters. Your body feels brittle and shaky from lack of sleep. Mario looks awful too. Now you'll have to carry Edik out of here.

'Saving Charlie was easy by comparison,' Mario chuckles. It's a weak joke, but at least he can still make one.

'This is the worst bit, now,' you say to Edik. 'I'm sorry.' You and Mario will have to drag him out from under the tree and onto the stretcher.

You each take Edik under an armpit.

'On three,' says Mario. 'One, two...'

Three. There's a scrape, a muffled howl – Edik's face pale and clenched, his legs dragging under the tree – then he's out. You lay him on the stretcher.

'I'm so sorry,' you say. 'It's over now – you're out.' Tears well up and spill down your cheeks as you check his legs. You loosen the tourniquets and no fresh blood wells. You pray Mr Ford does send out a team to find Edik as promised, with pain medicine or at least some fresh pairs of strong arms.

'They'll fly you to Sydney and operate on your legs,' Mario promises. 'It's amazing what doctors can do these days.'

Edik opens his eyes – they're a deep blue-grey, like stormy skies. Teodor's eyes are just the same shade. Edik reaches up and brushes your cheek with a rough finger. 'You... are an angel,' he whispers. 'I see angels all around. So beautiful.'

His words are lovely, but they frighten you, because you're not sure if he's starting to slip away into the afterlife. You grab the ends of the sapling stretcher and your palms sear with pain. You grit your teeth and lift. Mario does too.

You stumble onwards into the next phase of hell. Edik is out cold – only his noisy breathing gives you any reassurance – and damn it, he's heavy. At least with the daylight, navigating the bush has become a little easier, but that means you don't check the map and compass as often as you perhaps should. Also, you don't dare to stop and put Edik down.

You just keep on, despite your burning muscles, ragged dry throat and swirling vision.

Eventually, Mario stops behind you. You're in a gully thick with bush. 'How long has it been?' he begs, in a cracked voice.

You have no idea. 'Endless,' you mumble. You feel like you left Olenka's home a hundred years ago.

'Well, where are we on the map?' he asks.

'We'd better check,' you admit. Gently, you lower Edik to the ground. He stirs but doesn't wake. Your hands shake as you drag the map from your bag – you can barely control your fingers.

Your mind spins as you try to interpret the whorled circles of contour lines and the little blue and red threads of stream and road. *Admit it*, says a voice in your head, *you're lost*. You acknowledge that the voice is right: you've been blundering on with such single-minded determination that you've completely lost track of where you are. Your eyes cast about. *If this gully is that one, then we're behind that ridge...so if we cross it and then go over that saddle...*

You realise that on the left flank of the gully you're in now, there's an almost vertical climb over some boulders to the crest of the hill. If you're where you guess you are, then climbing up to the top should give you a view back to Cooma.

'I'm going to climb up there,' you say to Mario. But he has leant back against a tree and closed his eyes, oblivious. You're as exhausted as he is, and you know that it wouldn't be easy climbing the boulders even if you were feeling fresh and strong. Maybe it's not such a good idea after all. Edik moans something in Polish without opening his eyes. His face looks grey and his lips are pale and papery. You don't have much time left to save him.

Will you keep ploughing on in what you think is the right direction, or will you climb the boulders and check to be certain?

<hr />

✴ To continue in your current direction, go to page 184.

✴ To climb the boulders and check where you are, go to page 188.

Twenty minutes later, you stand in Olenka's kitchen again, still wearing your wet clothes, preparing her a cup of tea. *She won't taste it in the tea if you add some milk and sugar*, you remember Mr Ford instructing you.

You hesitate, your fingers holding the little white pill above the surface of the brown, steaming liquid.

This is for the best, you tell yourself. *It can't hurt her. It will just make her sleep really well, so that she feels better in the morning.*

Plip – the pill goes in. You poke it with a teaspoon and stir until it's all dissolved.

As you hand Olenka the tea, you feel a pang of guilt, but you dismiss it. She swallows it gratefully and sighs.

'Everything will be better in the morning,' you say. '*Pan Spycharka* said they'd have him back by lunchtime. And you know, Olenka, Mr Ford really didn't seem like a *spycharka* tonight. He was really concerned.'

Olenka nods slowly. Already, she's starting to sag.

'Come on,' you say, 'let's get you to bed.'

It's slightly warmer in the bedroom. You tuck

Olenka in next to her children. She shudders as all the tension she's been holding on to eases out of her body. 'If Edik die...' she murmurs.

'Edik won't die,' you reassure her.

You go back out into the lounge room and close the door to their bedroom to keep the heat in. You set up your bed on the couch, as you do every night. It's freezing out here. The room faces south, and the wind forces its way through every crack.

You take off your wet clothes. Your skin is covered in goosebumps and your fingertips are puckered and wrinkled with moisture. The dry clothes you put on cling to your damp skin, and you towel your hair vigorously, but even after you've climbed into bed, you still can't get warm. You wrap your blanket around yourself as tightly as an Egyptian mummy's bindings. Still you shiver.

You are too tired to get up and go outside to the woodheap, but too cold to fall asleep. Then you remember the kerosene heater in the kitchen cupboard. You drag it out and light it. Normally you wouldn't waste the fuel by leaving a heater running overnight, but tonight you really need it.

I'm going to wake up early in the morning and take the children so that Olenka can rest, you remind yourself. *I need a good sleep too.*

The bluish flames from the kerosene heater give

the room an eerie underwater light. You stuff your towel across the crack under the door to stop the draught, wanting the room to be toasty as an oven.

You climb back into bed and wait for the heater to work its magic. The room becomes steadily warmer, and your mind grows fuzzy. You fall asleep.

When you roll over a couple of hours later, you're aware of a pounding headache but you can't even sit up. You feel groggy and dizzy. The kerosene heater has made the room beautifully warm, but something's wrong. You want to sink back into sleep, but you feel nauseous and you're finding it harder to breathe.

Suddenly, you're seized with panic. With a flash of clarity, you remember: *Those heaters! They poison the air!*

You flail and fall off the couch. Then you look up at the pretty blue flames. You have no idea what you're doing there.

The room is lovely and warm. You sigh. Sleep will be so welcome. You rest your head on the floor and close your eyes.

THE END

✦ To return to the last choice you made and try again, go to page 146.

You almost blurt out, *I'd like to come on the tunnel inspection*, but then you decide you'll have more chance of success if you can make Mr Ford think it was *his* idea to take you. So instead you say: 'I'm glad I don't have to go! Is it all right if I take tomorrow's morning-tea rations back for the Nowak children?'

As you expected, making it sound like you're pleased to be able to shirk work and want to reapportion the food supplies puts Mr Ford on instant alert.

'Now that I think of it, we will need you to come,' he says. 'Arrive early to pack the morning-tea supplies in a hamper.'

You pretend to be reluctant, but inside you're dancing. You're going to see the project up close!

In the morning, you dress warmly and arrive early. You ride in the company jeep to the site where the new tunnel is being excavated. Mario is a tunneller – he's out at sites like this every day, so you haven't seen him for months, let alone thought about making up with him after your big argument. You can hear the tunnel before you see it: the clank of winches, the thrumming of drills, echoing from deep within the rock.

Mr Ford strides up to the tunnelling team leader, a tall man with a ginger beard who's left a small building near the tunnel entrance to meet you at your jeeps. 'Why haven't you stopped work, De Vries?' he demands. 'You knew there was an inspection scheduled for ten a.m.!'

Mr De Vries glances at his watch. 'But it's nine forty-five, sir,' he says in an accent you guess is Dutch.

'My watch says ten,' insists Mr Ford, without even looking at it. 'Order them to stop work now.' He turns away.

You glance at your own small watch. It is nine forty-five, for heaven's sake. Mr Ford would insist the earth were flat if it suited him. He thinks he's too important to wait for fifteen minutes, even when he's in the wrong. Without saying a word, you flash your watch at the tunnelling team leader. It seems to give him the gumption to stand up to Mr Ford.

'We're on track to break a new speed record for tunnelling, and I'm not going to stop the boys fifteen minutes early,' De Vries insists. 'We'll stop work, as requested, when *everybody's* watches say ten.'

Begrudgingly, Mr Ford looks at his own watch and realises he'd look petty to persist. 'Very well,' he says. 'We'll have our morning tea early.' He gestures to you to fetch the hamper.

Just as you turn back to the nearby jeep containing the hamper, you hear a rumbling boom issue from the mouth of the tunnel, followed by cracks and crunches. You spin to see a cloud of dust exhaling from the tunnel and De Vries running through it towards the entrance, throwing on his hard hat, and shouting back over his shoulder: 'Send help! Send help!'

Mr Ford swears and shakes his head, and his engineers just stand there, thunderstruck. Over at the small building near the tunnel's entrance, you see a man in overalls shouting into a two-way radio.

'What's happened?' you ask Mr Ford.

'A damned accident, I think,' he replies, looking more frustrated than worried. 'The workers drill long holes and pack them with dynamite to blast apart the rock. They're meant to drill new holes after each blast, but it saves time to drill back into what's left of the old holes, and sometimes there are traces of explosive still in there. The friction from the drill sets it off, and *boom.*'

You run to the man on the radio to see if you can do anything to help, but he waves at you to wait a minute. You see the clipboard of the day's roster on the desk, and your heart gives a lurch as you realise Mario might be in the tunnel. Sweat springs to your palms and your breathing quickens as you scan the list of names: Alexeev, Claesen, Castellanos, Davies,

De Luca – *oh no* – De Luca, Mario. *He's in there.*

You see a torch on the desk and grab it. There's also a white hard hat next to the clipboard, and you jam it onto your head. *Mario's life is in danger – he might even be dead – and I never apologised to him,* you think frantically as you run towards the tunnel.

Once inside, you can hear echoing moans. You start to shake, and the torchlight wobbles. *Keep calm,* you tell yourself. As the tunnel gets deeper and the darkness grows around you, you see two hunched figures emerging. It's the team leader, De Vries, and a wounded man you've never seen before, who is clutching at his stomach and spitting blood.

'Don't go in there!' De Vries cries. 'It's not stable!'

'My cousin's in there,' you say resolutely.

You start to run. Then your torchlight falls on a pile of rubble and twisted metal up ahead. Two men are bending over some figures on the ground. You can hear their voices clearly now:

'Come on, Sam…keep your hand on it and press hard…'

'It's all right, there's help coming…'

'Where's Petrov?'

As you run towards them, you hear a deep, ominous creak, and the walls seem to shudder. You swing your torch up and see a slab of rock overhead with a jagged crack across one corner. *It's not stable,*

De Vries said. You can't go any deeper into the tunnel now, not even for Mario – it's too dangerous. But you can help these men just ahead of you on your way out. You steel your nerves and dash towards them.

You reach the nearest fallen man and grab his ankles, saying to the closest worker bending over him: 'Grab his arms and let's get out of here.'

The worker's head snaps up at your voice, and although his face is blackened with grime, you suddenly see – *it's Mario!* Your heart leaps, but you both know you don't have time for a reunion; he just grins at you and scoops the injured man up by his armpits. You take one side, he takes the other, and you both stagger.

'How about this for a coincid—' Mario begins, but the air is torn by a huge *crack!* It's like a giant crunching bones for dinner. You have no time to run, or even react. The slab of rock overhead gives way under its own weight, cleaves from the rock above it, and drops, like a black foot stamping down on an insect. Death comes very quickly.

THE END

✦ To return to the last choice you made and try again, go to page 154.

You arrive at the office late, once you're sure everyone will have definitely left for the tunnel inspection. If anyone finds you here, though, you have an excuse: you've brought your English books along and will say you've come to study in peace.

The office is chilly – all the heaters that usually keep the room warm are off. Last night there was a raging storm, and Olenka's house was an icebox this morning. Olenka is happy, though, because Edik is in town for the next few days. In fact, he joined Mr Ford on the tunnel inspection today, because it's one of the sites he surveyed. He got home just before the storm hit last night with a hair-raising tale about nearly being hit by a falling tree.

You're not sure if it's the cold or the thrill of being a secretive student that gives your arms goosebumps as you open the filing cabinet next to Mr Ford's desk.

You examine a map you find that shows where the pipelines and power stations will be placed. The height the water has to fall governs how much energy is produced. You slowly follow the equations.

It seems like they use an equation that involves gravity, but the water isn't simply falling vertically – they have to consider how much friction there is in the pipe, which slows it down. It's like a trail of clues.

Once you understand what's happening, you try doing the calculations for one of the pipes yourself, and when you check their answer and see it matches your own, you get a tremendous rush of satisfaction.

These engineers are sculptors, you think. *They can take a messy hunk of nature and craft it into something smooth and synchronised, which will last for centuries.*

You start looking at the plans for two tunnels that are meant to meet up in the middle of a mountain. Each tunnel descends at a slightly different angle to meet at exactly the same spot below the earth. It looks neat on paper – the mountain like a cake sliced in half – but you know it must be difficult for the tunnellers to achieve in practice. This is one of the tunnels Mr Ford and his team are inspecting today.

Suddenly, you remember throwing out a blueprint like this that Mr Ford left scrunched up under his desk around two weeks ago. You wonder if it's still in the big bin of waste to be incinerated. Waste is only burnt fortnightly, so it may still be there. If you found it then you could compare the two and see if you could find the mistake that made him throw the other one away.

There it is! You retrieve the crumpled blueprint and spread it out on the table in the kitchenette. You make yourself a cup of tea (*milk, one sugar*) and drink it while you compare the two plans.

The blueprints look identical, except that the crumpled one has a big brown stain on it. You feel a bit deflated. It seems that the first blueprint was just thrown away because someone spilled their tea on it. Still, you decide to check if there are any other mistakes. You start by using trigonometry to check if all the angles add up. You soon notice that there is a tiny difference. The first, crumpled blueprint says that tunnel B needs to be drilled at an angle of twenty-six degrees, but on the second, it's written as twenty-nine degrees. Which one is right?

As you do the sums, a suspicion starts to grow inside you. Twenty-nine degrees can't be right. If they drill that steeply, then the tunnel will go too deep and will miss connecting with tunnel A by hundreds of metres!

You stop and take a deep breath. *Is it actually*

possible that someone has made an error when they've copied out this blueprint, and that I've just rescued the correct one from the bin?

You force yourself to think through this very carefully. If it turns out you're wrong, you'll have made yourself look stupid, and revealed to everyone that you were sneaking around the office today, and after that blow-up over Lidia, that will probably mean you'll be out of a job.

You do what an engineer would do. You triple-check everything. You consult the maps, and the surveyor's report, put together by a team of workers including Edik. By the time you've completed this meticulous work, you're certain that Mr Ford threw away the wrong blueprint. The one the tunnellers have been basing their work on is incorrect. A huge bubble of excitement swells your chest with pride. *Now I'll show them what I can do! They'll have to respect me now.*

YOU MANAGE TO find a lift with some workers and reach the mouth of the tunnel in record time. Looking down its yawning black throat, your heart hammers with excitement. When you hear a voice calling out for you to stop, you turn to see a wiry, grubby man in overalls, who must be one of the tunnellers.

'Oi! No women in the tunnels!' he cries.

'What?' You're flabbergasted. 'Why not?'

'Because it's terrible bad luck, that's why,' he asserts. 'No woman's ever been allowed down here, and they never will be. It'd cause a tunnel collapse, or some sort of disaster!'

You stare at him. *Why would people believe such nonsense? Next he'll accuse me of witchcraft!*

'But I have to take something to Mr Ford,' you tell him. 'It's very important!'

'You'll have to wait till he gets out,' the tunneller says stoutly.

'I can take it in to him,' a familiar voice offers behind you.

'Mario!' you cry. You haven't seen him since your argument when you first arrived.

'I'll look after it,' Mario says to his co-worker. 'Go and have your tea.'

The man shuffles off. You realise how glad you are to see Mario, and that your argument isn't important anymore – you just want your cousin to be your best friend again.

You give him a hug. 'Sorry,' you mumble.

'It was all my fault,' he replies. 'Friends?'

'Forever,' you affirm.

'I heard you were working for the big boss these days – but I can see you hadn't heard about the women in tunnels superstition.' Mario chuckles. 'Load of rubbish. Let's go.'

He leads you in to find Mr Ford and the others. This tunnel is nothing like Cat's Mouth: it's as wide and tall as a house, and reinforced on all sides with steel beams. Pipes go down the sides of the wall to carry fresh air deep underground, and train tracks run along the floor of the tunnel to bring workers and equipment in, and rubble out.

'It's hell down here when everything is running,' Mario tells you. 'There's noise like you wouldn't believe: rumbling, crashing, pounding. It's a relief to see daylight at the end of a shift.'

'I can believe it,' you say. Although the tunnel is an impressive feat of engineering, you do feel uneasy as you go further in. You never much liked being underground.

A few men are still working just inside the entrance, loading sections of enormous metal pipes onto canvas slings. Mario explains that the pipes will carry pressurised water, so they're extremely thick and heavy. Each piece is the size of a small car.

'We've all been asked to take a tea-break so the boss can come in, but we don't like to stop work for inspections; it slows us down,' Mario says. He explains that the tunnellers get extra pay if they break records for speed, so everyone is always striving their hardest. 'The problem is, you get so tired – and then you're more likely to have an accident. Last week I saw a man killed by a burst air pipe. It was lashing around like a whip.' He shudders, and so do you.

You walk down the sloping tunnel in silence after that, Mario's torchlight bobbing in front of you. The air is very still, and smells of rock dust. You feel Mario take your hand.

You explain to him how you think you've discovered a mistake in the blueprint. You're excited, but he's gutted. 'Weeks of work wasted because that fool threw out the wrong plan? And the little Italian tea-lady is the one who worked it out! That is *not* going to go down well. But you're a genius, of course – I always knew that, and now they will too.'

For the first time, you realise that you'll need to be discreet in how you point out this mistake. If you make Mr Ford look like an idiot in front of everyone, he'll get defensive.

You hear voices up ahead. *That's them!* Your heart

starts to clatter. Here you are, deep underground on one of the most ambitious engineering projects the world has ever seen, making your contribution. Mr Ford is just ahead, with two workers from the office, taking measurements and making notes.

When he sees you, his brow furrows in confusion. 'What are you doing here?'

'Sir, can I have a quiet word?'

'Certainly not. We're in the middle of an inspection!' He looks around. 'Who brought the tea-lady?'

'Mister Ford, I know I'm the tea-lady, but I'm also very good at maths,' you argue. 'I was in the office today and—' You begin to get out the documents, but Ford snatches them away from you.

'Those are confidential!' he snaps.

'Please, Mr Ford,' you beg. You're getting desperate. 'You have to listen to me! The tunnels won't meet! You threw out the wrong plan!'

'Get her out of here,' he snaps and turns his back. But Mario stands his ground.

'She says she found a mistake, and I believe her,' he states. 'None of us will go back to work on this tunnel until you've checked it.'

Mr Ford exhales through his teeth. He snatches the papers and orders one of his assistants to hold them up while he inspects them by torchlight.

'It's a difference of three degrees, sir,' you point out. 'Just there.'

You hear him swear under his breath. 'Fitzsimmons, Schmid,' he commands, 'meeting outside. And go and get Edik Nowak – he's further down the tunnel.' He turns on his heel and begins to walk away.

I was right, you think. *I knew it!* You're going to go to this meeting that Mr Ford wants to hold outside, and you're going to join in. This is your foot in the door – you just have to keep your nerve and stay respectful.

You become aware of a distant sound like a tolling bell, clanging and echoing. 'Do they ring a bell for lunch here?' you ask Mario. He shakes his head, and the sound grows louder – it's not rhythmical, it's more of a jangling, bashing noise, like Teodor might make on one of Olenka's cooking pots. And now you can hear metallic squeals and dry, rocky crunches too.

'The pipe!' Mario shouts. 'There's a pipe coming down. Get back, get back!'

You look back and see Mr Ford and his two co-workers leap into an alcove in the side of the tunnel. Mario hesitates for a split second, clearly wondering whether he can reach the alcove too before the runaway pipe does. But you know that Edik is deeper into the tunnel, and you can see some large waste skips further down the track with enough clearance for you to slide in underneath, so you sprint towards the skips, screaming Edik's name. Mario sprints after you.

The noise sounds like some demon is wielding the metal pipe in a fury. You hope that the pipe will just glance off the skips and go over the top, or to one side. The safest place to be is under them. You run as hard as you can, limbs burning, urging your body faster and faster. You dive as you reach the closest skip and scramble under, scraping and bumping yourself on the ground. Mario fits in beside you and wraps his arms around you.

But where is Edik? You scream his name and look out down the tracks to see a figure running towards you. It's him! He's going to make it!

Everything happens in an instant. You feel a wall of air push against you. Mario squeezes you from behind, hard. Edik dives towards your skip and hits the ground. You shoot out an arm to help pull him under. He grabs it with both of his. The last thing you see before the pipe hits and you shut your eyes tight is his terrified eyes, glowing white in the gloom; he hasn't made it under the skip.

The skip, packed with rock, gives a bone-shaking jerk as the pipe slams into it, and shards of rock fly about like shrapnel. You hear a horrible shriek as the pipe ricochets to the side of the skip. You hold fast to Edik's hands, and you're still trying with all your strength to drag him to safety when the sharp edge of the metal pipe rips past the side of the skip and into your arm.

For a split second that feels like eternity, you are thrown onto your back by a tidal wave of agony. You scream at the underside of the skip, feel Mario's hands scrabble for you in the darkness. You throw your head from side to side, sucking air in through your clenched teeth and letting it out in throat-shredding howls. You clutch at your shoulder and feel something warm and sticky. Your heart ratchets up to a frantic staccato. Nausea and sweat flood your body. Just when you're certain that you can't take anymore, a sweet dark fog rolls through you. Gasping with relief, your muscles go loose and you pass out.

✦ Go to page 191.

You look at the boulders again. *No, climbing up there would be too risky,* you decide. You're so exhausted you can barely keep your balance on flat ground, let alone dozens of metres above the ground.

You shake Mario's shoulder and he stumbles upright again. Together, you brace yourselves and pick up the stretcher once more. Edik opens his eyes with a little gasp as you lift him off the ground.

'Edik, how are you going?' you ask. 'Be strong; not far to go now.'

'*Chcę, żebyś mnie pochował nad brzegiem Narwi,*' he mumbles.

'Can you say it in English?' you ask.

'Bury me ... Narew River ...' he murmurs. 'My home.'

'Edik, you won't be buried anytime soon,' says Mario, too cheerily. You exchange fearful glances.

Where is this rescue party? you think. *The one Mr Ford was going to send. Please!*

You force one foot in front of the other, praying that you interpreted the map correctly and that soon, this gully will end. In about a kilometre, you should see a break in the ridgeline where you can cross through to Cooma.

It doesn't come. *Has it been a kilometre? Should I stop and check the map again?* Doubts run through your mind. *I'm such an idiot – why are we trying to carry him out at all? It would have been better to stay where we dug him out and wait for help…*

He's not going to make it.

I'm not going to make it.

You stumble on a rock and bash your knee, hard. Edik nearly slides off the stretcher. You right yourself just in time, but now you're hobbling.

This is futile. I want to stop. I have to stop.

'We have to rest,' says Mario in a hoarse whisper behind you. 'We're lost… aren't we?'

'No!' you choke. You want to cry, but there's no moisture left for tears. 'Cooma's just… just…' You're nodding your head to the left, where you pray it is.

'But if the sun goes down in the west… doesn't that mean now we're going… south?' he asks.

'I don't know, Mario!' you cry. It comes out like a bleat. 'Why don't you work it out yourself, like I'm trying to?'

'Because I don't have the brains,' he says bitterly. 'I have good luck, that's it – or at least, I used to—' He breaks off with a gasp and cries out: 'Stop!' You glance back at him. 'Snake!' he screams, just as your foot falls.

You leap backwards as the snake's head whips through the air and strikes you between the top of your sock and your trouser cuff. There's a strong sting, like a wasp bite, and then the snake flashes like a brown ribbon through the undergrowth and is gone.

You and Mario lower Edik to the ground, and you start to sob. You clutch at your leg, squeezing it hard, to try to stop the venom passing through your body. Mario is ripping off his singlet and binding it tightly around your lower leg, swearing under his breath in a constant stream.

The bite now feels like a throbbing ball of flame. The pain makes you want to faint. 'I'm going to die,' you whisper.

'No, no, it hurts, but not all snake bites are venomous,' Mario says, hugging you to him, but there is real terror in his voice as he screams, 'Help! Somebody…help!'

You're starting to shiver, and your head hurts. Mario squeezes you tight, and a few moments later you heave and vomit all over his legs. Your stomach hurts, and you taste blood.

Mario doesn't let you go even for a moment. 'Don't leave me,' he whispers in your ear. 'Please, don't leave me!'

You have a blinding headache behind your eyes, so awful that it feels like someone has crammed the sun inside your brain. You forget about Edik, and Olenka, and the children. You forget that you're in Australia; that you came from Italy. The venom leaps from thought to thought, until you *are* the pain, and the pain is you, hurtling down a long black tunnel.

You have one last sensation: arms are holding you. Your first and last friend, Mario. His name reaches your lips in a whisper. Then it's gone.

THE END

✦ To return to your last choice and try again, go to page 164.

You don't know where you're going to get the strength from, but you'll have to climb those boulders. The thought of bashing on through the bush for hours in the wrong direction is too awful to contemplate.

Come on, legs, you tell them, *go!*

You scramble up the foothill, then start to climb, carefully testing each foothold and handhold before you commit to it. Sometimes the rocks wobble with a deep, hollow sound like a drum. You notice lichen and little ants all over the rocks, and wiry grasses clinging to thin wedges of dirt.

You're pleased with how well you're climbing. You look back: Mario and Edik are a long way down. *Not far to go*, you tell yourself. You feel a little bubble of hope rise in your chest as you approach the crest of the ridge. *If I'm right*, you tell yourself, *then down there will be...* You draw a deep breath and heave yourself up the last rock... *Cooma! Yes!*

The twinkle of glass and metal, and the cleared brown strips around the town, never looked so welcoming. *We're on the right track home*, you congratulate yourself. *Edik's going to make it.*

'See, Mamma?' you say out loud. 'I did it!'

Then you laugh at yourself. *You can cross the world*, you think ruefully, *but you still just want to show off to your mamma.*

There's no sign of the rescue party, so you clamber to your feet to try shouting for them. *They could just about hear me in Cooma from here*, you think. Even though you're within striking distance of home, it would be great not to have to carry Edik any further.

The moment you get to your feet, you realise you've made a mistake. There's a scraping groan that seems to come from underground, and an ominous shifting underfoot. You try to spring sideways to a bigger boulder, but before you can push off, your rock slips. You plummet backwards and land hard, upside down. The rocks under you shift and you start to slide. Loose rocks are bouncing down the hill, cracking and smashing into others. You wrap your arms over your head but you keep sliding, faster and faster. You're being knocked and scraped as you struggle to slow down.

Suddenly, to your right, you see a huge jutting rock. Your arm shoots out and your shoulder wrenches, but you manage to grab the rock, and it holds fast. You scrabble for traction, and with a gasp of relief you realise you're no longer falling.

Then you see a boulder hurtling towards you. It's the size of a small table. You wrap your other arm over your head and duck, still holding tightly to the rock. You hear Mario's scream far below, and the thunderous cracks of the boulder as it ricochets off other rocks.

The boulder smashes into the rock you're clinging to. Pain like nothing you've ever felt before rips through you with the force of a hurricane. The tall rock was strong enough to halt the boulder's progress, and your arm is pinned between them. You scream and fight, your body crackling with panic, pushing at the boulder, but you may as well be an ant.

The pain of your crushed arm engulfs your whole body. You can't think, can't speak, can only shriek and howl like an animal. A swell of dizziness rises up and swallows you. You pass out.

✦ Go to page 191.

You wake up. Blink. You're somewhere sunny... in a bed. White sheets. Hushed sounds. You slide back into sleep.

It's night. Footsteps pass by your bed. You close your eyes and are dimly aware of someone checking your breathing and pulse, touching your left hand gently, and moving away again. You sleep.

Now, the honeyed light of late afternoon, warm in a square on your thighs. You blink. 'Hello there,' says a voice tenderly. The room swims into focus. By your bedside is someone with messy dark hair, kind eyes, and that moustache...

'Mario,' you whisper.

You feel him touch your face. 'You made it,' he murmurs.

'I did?' *Where did I make it?* you wonder. *Where was I before this?* You cast your mind back. You remember normal life in Cooma, and then... there's nothing. A black void where memory should be.

You notice tears on Mario's cheeks. You haven't seen him cry since he was a small boy. You feel worried. 'I'm okay,' you whisper. 'Aren't I?'

'Yes, of course you're okay,' he rushes to assure you. 'You're … you're great, you're alive – that's all that matters.'

'I'm so sleepy,' you murmur.

Mario brushes your hair back from your brow. 'Then rest,' he says quietly. 'I'll be here when you wake up.'

Night. You wake from a strange dream. Moonlight shines through a chink in the curtains. You try to roll over to your right side. You push with your left arm, reach out with your right – but something's wrong. You can feel your right shoulder and upper arm, but nothing more. You look down and see a strange white shape in the moonlight. Your arm – it stops in a bandaged stump like a zucchini. There's no elbow, no arm, no hand. Panic washes through you. *This must be part of my bad dream.*

'Help!' you shout in a cracked voice. Footsteps come running. You reach down to touch the end of your right arm – it's a dense, neatly wrapped package budding from your shoulder. '*Help!*' you scream, your voice rising to true horror. You scrabble to get out of bed. Your heart is stammering.

A nurse grabs your shoulders and presses you back onto the bed. 'It's all right, calm down,' she commands.

Your whole body is shaking. You start screaming. *Wake up, wake up, wake up!* you implore yourself.

'You'll wake the others,' the nurse hisses. You gulp for air. 'That's quite enough,' she says firmly. You feel her push open your mouth and place a tablet on your tongue. She raises your head with one hand and lifts a glass of water to your lips. 'Swallow.' You do. She puts your head back on the pillow and tucks the sheets so tightly around you that you can barely wriggle.

You lie quietly, sobbing in the darkness, not understanding what is going on or how to make it stop. Slowly, the pill works and a cool calmness slides through you. Your brain goes fuzzy and the room starts to swim. You sleep again.

YOU'RE AWAKE. *Is it morning? It's cloudy today. There's Mario.*

'Hug me,' you whisper, and he does. You feel a warm rush of gratitude that he's there, warm and solid. You let out a shaky breath. 'I had the most horrible dream,' you tell him. You still feel sick with the memory of it. A shudder runs through you and he squeezes you tighter. You squeeze him back, but through the haze of your doped-up groggy thoughts you begin to realise that you're only holding him with your left arm. You try to lift your right. All you feel is pain shooting through your shoulder.

'Don't move too much,' Mario says. 'You've been out for days.'

You know why you're in the hospital now. Last night wasn't a nightmare.

'It's gone…isn't it?' you mumble. 'My arm.'

You no longer feel panic, but an all-pervasive sense of doom – a certainty that nothing will ever be right again.

Mario doesn't say yes or no. 'You were so brave,' he murmurs. 'You were amazing.' He draws back from the hug. You look at your right arm. The bandages. The space where you end. The realisation is a kick in the guts.

You can't cry. You are too stunned. Three nurses swarm in for your check-up, and now that you are properly awake for the first time, they have lots of questions for you.

'What do you remember about the accident?'

'On a scale of one to ten, how much pain are you in?'

'What year is it?'

'How many fingers am I holding up?'

Their questions are exhausting and stupid, and

although your brain takes longer than usual to think and reply in English, you're able to answer all of the questions except one: 'What do you remember about the accident?'

After they leave, you sit quietly, thinking about each of the events leading up to the blank hole in your memory. You follow the day's events like a thread, getting closer and closer to the trauma, when suddenly you gasp: 'Edik!'

Mario's eyes snap to your face.

'That's what I was doing – trying to save Edik!' you exclaim. Mario doesn't say a word. He doesn't need to. His face is grey and wretched.

'He...didn't make it?' you stammer. *Oh God, please tell me he's alive. Tell me it wasn't for nothing. If he lived but I lost my arm, that's a fair trade. Please, God, please.*

Mario shakes his head. It's as if a trapdoor opens in your chest and you fall through into an endless black hole. You hear Mario saying, 'His injuries...they tried but...he died. The funeral was two days ago.'

You can't face him. You roll away and bury your head in the pillow, your eyes shut tight, as if they could keep out the whole world. *Olenka. I failed her. Lidia and Teodor don't have a father now.*

You feel Mario's hand on your shoulder. 'You were a hero,' he insists, but the word sounds hollow and ugly. You just pretend to be asleep, until finally he leaves you alone.

You know for sure now that you were wrong all this time – the curse is real. It has always been real, and your attempts to live your life as if you were in control were ridiculous. You now understand exactly how Mamma felt: you're in the grip of a power far greater than you are. Other people around you go on living their carefree lives, deluding themselves that they are free to make their own choices. But the curse breeds in you like black mould. It will be with you for the rest of your life, and it's all you deserve.

OLENKA AND THE children don't come. You suppose they loathe you, or worse, pity you. You have weird sensations that your missing limb is still there: sometimes it aches so badly that you cry in the night; sometimes it feels like the fingers you don't have are being pierced by burning needles. For over twelve hours, at one stage, you are bedevilled by an itch in your non-existent right elbow. You punch and scratch the space on your bed where your arm should be, but the ghost-arm doesn't feel that.

Paradoxically, the nurses give you real painkillers to combat the phantom pain, and it actually works, at least for the first hour or two.

Mario cheers little milestones, like the first time you sit up in bed; the first time the drip comes out of your arm; the first time you stand and then walk. But life beyond the hospital is impossible to imagine. You don't see how a one-armed person could ever work, or marry, or be anything but a burden to others. *It would have been better if I had died*, you think.

'I haven't told anyone at home what happened yet,' Mario tells you. 'Do you want me to?'

'No,' you reply. 'Mamma was right about the curse all along.' Mario strokes your left arm. 'I suppose I'll have to go home,' you mumble. 'Another problem for her to deal with.'

Mario looks at you severely. 'Now, stop that,' he commands. 'You're not a problem. You're not cursed. It's amazingly good luck that you're alive at all!'

'I disagree.'

You see tears well in Mario's eyes. 'There's still a life for you here,' he insists. 'I'll help!' When you don't reply, he goes on: 'You lost your arm. Not your brain, or your heart – not any of the things that make you so special. We'll get through this together.'

Mario's words, his tears, and his offers of help

only confirm your worst fears. 'I'm making you feel bad,' you mutter. 'Olenka can't face me either – I'm just salt in her wound.'

Mario is openly crying now. You roll away from him, curled up in shame. 'I want to convince you,' he chokes, 'that life is still worth living.'

'You can't,' you state. You are filled with a black, writhing guilt. You didn't save Edik. You have wrecked the lives of all those who loved you. Your family will never be free of you: every day for the rest of your life, you will need help with the smallest things. At the root of this anguish is the knowledge that you brought it all upon yourself: you stole the golden cornetto, which was the cornerstone of your family's fortune. You ripped it out, and everything came crashing down. Where would you all be now if you had never touched it?

The next day, Mario comes in very early. 'I'm starting back at work,' he tells you, 'so I won't see you until dinnertime. But I think you'll have some other visitors today.'

Around eleven o'clock, you're sitting up in bed when Olenka shuffles in, without her children. It's a punch in the chest to see the state of her. She was so strong, so capable; she'd escaped the war, and started a new life in a place where she couldn't speak the language, but she never complained, always striving towards a brighter future. Now, her hair is lank and her shoulders slope as though they've finally given up taking the weight of the world. When she smiles at you, it seems as though the corners of her mouth are lifted by little strings, not by any real feeling.

You know what that's like. You've been 'smiling' at people like that all week.

'Hello,' you say to her quietly, as she sits by your bedside. 'You don't need to smile. I don't feel like it either.'

Olenka gives a shaky, relieved sigh. 'I walk, I smile,' she says croakily. 'But is … show only.'

You thought it would be unbearable to look at Olenka's face; to see the suffering written there. But now her hazel eyes look into yours without flinching – the eyes of someone who has dived down and touched the bottom of sorrow, and is still swimming back up for air – and you realise she knows how you feel. She doesn't say anything to try to make it better. The cracks in her heart mirror the cracks in yours.

You feel a deep love towards her, broken as she is, and some of that love reflects back and warms you. Then, gradually, something profound shifts in you. Grief is running in like a tide. You're not numb anymore. Tears come at last.

You let yourself cry, and Olenka cries too. You mourn for Edik, for her children, for the arm that will never come back. You remember the accident, and your sobs become deeper as you realise that it wasn't your fault – there was nothing anyone could have done. Eventually Olenka leans forward, presses her damp cheek to yours, and sighs a kiss.

'I love you,' you tell her.

'I love you too,' she replies.

'Why … why didn't you come sooner?'

She looks down for a moment. 'I am not want … to hurt you. You … nearly die to save Edik. If I come and cry here, I am insult to you. I am problem for you. So … I came to smile. My plan is to smile. But … I cry instead.' She shrugs.

You give her a real smile, and it feels wonderful. 'Thank you … for helping me cry,' you tell her.

There's a squeal at the doorway, then Lidia rushes in. A nurse follows with Teodor in her arms.

'Someone couldn't wait outside any longer,' the nurse says, nodding at Lidia.

'That's all right,' you say. 'Seeing them is the best medicine.' Lidia piles onto your lap and Olenka says something in Polish, which you take to be a caution to Lidia to be gentle.

'It's all right,' you say, and tousle Lidia's sweet

brown curls. She smiles brightly. Then her eyes widen as she sees your stump.

'That's where your arm…got off?' she says. She reaches out and brushes the bandages gently with her fingertips. You love the Australian twang in her voice when she speaks English: 'off' sounds like 'orf'.

'Yeah, mate,' you say in your best Aussie accent. 'That's where it god orf.'

Like a passenger getting off a train, you think, and you start to giggle.

Lidia looks astonished, then she grins and burrows her head into your chest for a hug. You squeeze her with your left arm and give her a little tickle. Her chuckle is the best sound in the world. You look over at Olenka, and she's smiling, really smiling. Life has returned.

YOU'VE BEEN GIVEN a plastic arm to wear, which is uniformly pink and smooth as a doll's arm. Its fingers don't move. Its elbow is at a permanent ninety-degree angle.

'You won't need to be here much longer,' the nurse tells you one morning. 'You're ready to tackle the world outside! Now' – she tightens the leather straps over your stump – 'how does that feel?'

'Like there's a heavy lump of plastic hanging off my stump,' you tell her honestly, and she cocks her head sympathetically.

'Well, you don't have to wear it,' she says, 'but it might be useful once you learn how to use it.'

There is obviously some meaning of the word 'useful' I've never heard before, you think, but instead you just nod, smile as she bustles off, and then unbuckle it. It lies on your bed like a magician's prop.

Hearing heavy footsteps, you look up with a start. Mr Ford is standing at the foot of your bed. Your stomach clenches.

This is all his fault, you think. *Edik's death, my arm…*

Then a voice inside you says: *No, he couldn't have foreseen this.*

Although you've never liked the man, you sense that dwelling on blame will hurt you more than it will hurt him. And he looks, you have to admit, cowed. He's holding his hat in his hands. He can't look you in the eye.

'Yes?' you say, and he startles, chews his lip.

'I'm sorry,' he begins, 'for the intrusion and, ah… your loss.'

'Why don't you sit down?' you say.

He perches awkwardly at your bedside and holds

up a clipboard. 'I'm here with...paperwork,' he fumbles. 'The documentation surrounding Edik's passing. It would really help if you can tell me everything you remember.' He coughs.

'Would you like a glass of water?'

He nods and reaches for the water jug on your bedside table, then leaps up as if stung, crying: 'Good God!' His chair topples backwards and clatters to the floor. He is gulping like a fish.

You examine your bedside table to see what could have caused such a reaction. There's your water jug, a newspaper, a medal that Lidia made you from a milk-bottle lid with the word 'BRAEVRY' scratched into it, and Charlie's compass, which survived the accident with only a small scratch and dent.

'Where did you get that?' he gasps.

'Uh, Lidia made it for me—'

'No – the compass! My compass!'

You stare at him. 'That's Charlie's compass – Charlie Sanders. He was a navigator for the—'

'I know who he was,' Mr Ford cuts across me. 'He's my brother. Or, I should say, he *was* my brother.'

Your mouth hangs open in disbelief. *This can't be! It must be a joke.* You examine Mr Ford's face. You can't get your head around the idea that this brutish man is Charlie's brother. *Impossible!* Before you can find any words, the impact of Mr Ford's *was* hits you.

'You mean...' you whisper, '...Charlie's dead?'

'Yes,' sighs Mr Ford, and you feel your heart shatter. 'I'm afraid so.'

'He was my teacher,' you tell him through tears. 'And my friend. I never would have come to Australia if not for him – and nor would my cousin, Mario.'

Realisation dawns on Mr Ford's face. 'You're the two he spoke of! The girl and boy who found him and hid him in the caves! You saved his life.' There's a pause. 'He thought that *you*, in particular, were a genius. Never met anyone like you, he said.'

You're stunned. To have come all this way, and find that Charlie's brother was right here under your nose the whole time!

'So, Charlie made it home from the war?' you ask.

'Yes, yes,' says Mr Ford, and then his face seems to close over. 'But things weren't right for him after that. He... died soon after. Anyway, we're here to talk about the incident,' he says briskly. 'What do you remember?'

You sense that Mr Ford is not being wholly truthful. *I'll get it out of you*, you think. *What aren't you telling me about Charlie?*

You tell Mr Ford about the events leading up to the

accident in as much detail as you can manage, though you hate to think about it. You still have nightmares, and the phantom pains and itches in your missing limb still plague you. 'That's all I can tell you,' you conclude, and Mr Ford closes his clipboard and stands up. Then his hand hovers over the compass.

'May I take this?' he asks. 'I'll return it.'

You are instantly suspicious. 'Why?'

He looks shifty. 'It's a memento, that's all. I'm sentimental.'

'No, you're not,' you counter. 'I know that much about you. Why do you want it?'

'All right.' He sighs. Then he takes a step closer and speaks in a hushed tone: 'It has a code on it – the combination code for a safe deposit box my father left in the Canberra bank that I've never been able to open. Charlie didn't know that when he gave it away.'

You're curious. You've had that compass for half your lifetime, and the only markings on it are the 'C' and the 'D' for 'Charlie' and 'Desmond'.

Mr Ford's eyes are drawn back to the compass. He picks it up and turns it over in his fingertips. 'Nothing visible externally...' he mutters. 'The code must be inside or else be some kind of puzzle...'

You hold out your hand. 'Mr Ford,' you say politely, 'that's my compass.'

Reluctantly, he puts it in your palm, clears his throat and shifts from side to side. You can tell he's itching to grab it and run, but you hold it tightly.

Eventually, he speaks. 'I can tell I've underestimated you, and I'm sorry,' he says. 'Would you consider taking up an apprenticeship as an engineer in my office? We'll pay for your university studies. Your handicap wouldn't be a problem.'

Up until five minutes ago, you considered the mere fact that I was a woman to be an insurmountable handicap, you think bitterly. *An engineering apprenticeship is what I've always wanted, and you know it. What are you up to, Desmond Ford?*

'Of course,' he goes on, 'as I would be entrusting you with such a great responsibility, I would expect in return that you would trust me enough to lend me the compass. I'll return it to you, of course, as soon as I figure out the code.'

You pause. 'What's in the safe, anyway?' you ask him.

He shrugs. 'I wish I knew,' he says. 'I only found out it existed when I read the letter my father left for me after he died. He told me that the contents of that bank safe were his greatest legacy, and that the code was engraved on my mother's heirloom compass. He thought Charlie still had it, of course.' He snorts.

'Dad always loved puzzles and mysteries. Sometimes I imagine him laughing at me from beyond the grave. I think he did it just to torture me.'

He really doesn't know what's in there, you think. *That's the bit he's being honest about. But there's something funny about the way he clammed up when I wanted to know about Charlie. What happened to Charlie?*

You consider what you will say to Mr Ford. You could say: *I'll give you the compass, but only if you tell me what really happened to Charlie. And I'll start as an apprentice engineer next Monday, thank you.*

Or, you could tell him to get lost. If there's a mysterious code on that compass, you want to find it – although you don't know how to find the safe, and the fortune wouldn't be rightfully yours, anyway. You'd also lose your best shot at finally getting your dream job.

Mr Ford holds out his hand.

✴ If you accept Mr Ford's offer and let him take the compass, go to page 208.
✴ If you keep the compass and refuse Mr Ford's offer, go to page 217.

You hold the compass over Mr Ford's outstretched palm. He smiles greedily. 'I'll lend it to you on the condition,' you say, 'that you tell me the truth about Charlie, and bring me a formal offer of the apprenticeship.'

'Visiting hours are over!' calls the nurse. Mr Ford takes the compass. 'Tomorrow,' he promises. 'Your new job, in writing.'

'And Charlie!' you call to his retreating back.

Darn it, that was dumb, you think. *Who's to say he'll ever come back with the job offer – let alone the truth? I just gave away my bargaining power.*

Still, whatever happens next, you feel ready to go out and tackle the world again, even if you need to do it single-handedly. You chuckle at your own pun. You're sure things will be frustrating at first as you adjust, and tiring, but you're so glad you're still alive.

The next morning – the day you're due to be discharged – the same nurse who was on duty yesterday, a short, wiry British woman called Nurse Ellis, hands you a manila envelope. You rip it open eagerly. The letter inside says: 'The Snowy

Mountains Hydro Electric Authority offers you a part-time engineering apprenticeship in combination with part-time university study, all tuition fees paid.' Who would have thought that losing your arm would give you this opportunity? You ask Nurse Ellis for a pen and sign the offer left-handed. That's a skill you'll have to work on.

Nurse Ellis doesn't seem particularly happy for you, though. 'Been making friends with Mr Ford then, have we?' she asks, and her tone is curt, like there's a bad taste in her mouth. She seems to think you've done a deal with the devil.

You look at her, puzzled. It's really none of her business, and you have half a mind to tell her that – but then again, perhaps she has a good reason to behave in this way.

'Why shouldn't I work for him?' you ask.

'He's a powerful man, I'm sure you'll go a long way,' she replies. Then she turns to walk away.

'Wait!' you cry. Nurse Ellis turns. 'Is there something I should know? Is this offer I just signed not real?'

Nurse Ellis chews her lip, as if making up her mind whether or not to speak. 'The offer's probably fine,' she says. 'I just don't think it's right... to disown your own brother like that.'

'What do you mean?' you ask.

'Charlie Sanders isn't dead. I should know – I was his nurse in Canberra Hospital until just last month, before I came here.'

'Charlie's alive?' you gasp. 'But why is he in hospital?'

'He's not right in the head,' Nurse Ellis says, tapping her temple. 'A lot of them after the war had reactions to the stress of war. Can't forget the awful things they've seen, can't adjust to normal life. Still, that Mr Ford should've taken care of his brother, not chucked him in a ward and thrown away the key.'

There's a long silence, in which you're too stunned to speak.

'I know some people are ashamed when a relative starts acting crazy,' she says eventually. 'A lot of people on that psych ward have been abandoned. But you *can* get better from these things – combat stress reaction, depression, you know. If you're treated with respect and loving kindness.'

She sighs.

'Anyway, that has nothing to do with your contract,' she goes on, in a lighter tone. 'Chance of a lifetime, if you like that kind of thing – as long as you don't mind being the only female engineer in the country!' She laughs.

'Thanks,' you say absently, but your insides have turned to jelly. Charlie's alive! You're delighted, but it's scary to think of him in a psychiatric ward. *If I go to visit him, will he still be Charlie?* you ask yourself. *Or has he changed into some sort of... beast?* You wonder what awful things happened to him after he disappeared mysteriously from the cat's guts all those years ago. Was he captured? Tortured? Poor Charlie.

You agree with Nurse Ellis that whatever state Charlie's in now, it's wrong for Mr Ford to pretend his brother is dead. A thought strikes you. 'If there were some sort of a fortune,' you begin, 'I mean, a will or an inheritance for both brothers... would Charlie get his share?'

'Not until he's discharged,' Nurse Ellis tells you. 'And Mr Ford would have to sign the papers for that.' She smiles sadly. 'Charlie's been in there for a long time, love. I remember when the family farm was sold against his will. He cried like a baby; said he felt so helpless.'

You remember the article you saw in *Truth* – Charlie's family farm was sold to Bob Dawe. It's another thing you'll have to ask Mr Ford about.

'In the eyes of the law,' Nurse Ellis goes on, 'once you're not of sound mind, you have limited rights. If there's a fortune, Mr Ford will likely get to control it all.'

Picking up your contract, you use your left hand and your teeth to rip it in two. It's time to leave this hospital once and for all. 'I'm going to Canberra,' you tell her.

While you dress one-handed (buttons are tricky; shoelaces are awful), you think about that golden compass. Charlie wouldn't have given it away if he'd known about the safe combination being on there. But what could the code be? The only markings on it were the 'C' and 'D' inside a circle, for 'Charlie' and 'Desmo'—

Wait! You stop mid-breath and drop your shoe. *I've got it!* Just then, Mario walks in. You barrel across the room and grab him by the shoulder. 'That's it!' you cry.

'Uh … hello to you too,' he begins.

'The "C" and the "D" don't stand for "Charlie" and "Desmond"!'

Mario just stares at you.

'They stand for "Circumference" and "Diameter"!' you crow. 'And the circumference of a circle divided by the diameter is always equal to …'

'I have no idea what you're talking about,' he confesses.

'It's equal to pi! The impossible, never-ending number! Three point one four one five nine two six five three five nine—'

'Stop, stop,' demands Mario. 'What the hell?'

'Oh, it's so simple!' you exclaim.

'Whatever's going on here,' says Mario, 'it's *not* simple. Have you lost your mind?'

'No!' you cry. 'I'll explain everything on the way to Canberra. Come on, you're driving me.' Mario bought a car while you were in hospital, which you thought was extravagant at the time, but now you're glad of it.

Mario trails in your wake. At the hospital's front door, you meet Olenka.

'Help me talk some sense into her,' Mario begs Olenka, gesturing at you. 'She's gone crazy!' He tries to explain what's going on to Olenka as they follow you outside, because you're not stopping for anything.

The trees in the gardens have grown their new spring leaves and the air is fresh and clean. You break into a run. You feel amazing, like you could fly.

'Which way's your car?' you shout, turning back to look at Mario, then – *smack* – you run straight into Mr Ford.

'Out for a run?' he asks, amused, then he looks at your face. What does he see there – wildness, triumph? Whatever it is, he steps back, unnerved. 'Hold it right there,' he says. 'Where are you going?'

You size him up. *You think you're so powerful, Mr Ford. Controlling everyone. But not me.*

'I'm going to visit Charlie,' you say and watch his face collapse. 'The brother you'd rather pretend was *dead* than admit is in a mental hospital.' Behind you, you hear Mario and Olenka gasp.

'It's not like that,' Mr Ford blusters. 'You don't understand…'

'You'd be surprised what I understand, Mr Ford,' you tell him.

You try to get past him, but he sidesteps and blocks you. 'You've worked it out,' he says, and his voice is suddenly hoarse. 'The code. Haven't you?' You notice the dark rings under his eyes; he must have stayed up all night trying to crack it. 'Why else would you be going to see Charlie?'

'Well, I don't know,' you say sarcastically. 'How about because I care about him? Because I want the best for him? Because I *love* him like family?'

Mr Ford grabs your hand in both of his. 'Tell me – tell me the code!' he begs. 'Please! It's not because I'm greedy – I'll share it with Charlie, whatever's in that safe! It's just...' He gives a shaky sigh and lets go, abashed. 'It's the last link I have with my father.'

You look at him sceptically. 'From the way you've treated Charlie, I wouldn't have guessed family meant so much to you.'

Mr Ford gives a deep, groaning sigh that seems to shake his very bones.

Then Olenka speaks up. Her voice is trembling, but there is steel in her eyes. 'If family important for you, Mr Ford, then why you never say sorry for Edik?'

There is a long silence. Mr Ford stands like a rock – apart from his slightly quaking shoulders. *Is he crying?* you wonder, astonished.

Mario passes him a handkerchief, and Mr Ford clutches at it. When he looks up, his eyes are rimmed with red. 'Olenka,' he says, 'I am so very sorry.'

Then he turns to you. 'I can change,' he says. 'I can be the brother I should have been to Charlie. I'll come to Canberra and prove it. Just tell me the code.'

You don't answer him straight away. You look at Mario and Olenka. They shrug as if to say: *It's your choice.*

It is my choice, you think. *Whatever life throws at me, I still get to choose how I respond.*

✳ If you keep the code to yourself and leave Mr Ford in Cooma, go to page 224.

✳ If you agree to tell Mr Ford the code and let him come to Canberra with you, go to page 227.

✳ To read a fact file about mental health and treatment, go to page 270, then return to this page to make your choice.

'No,' you say. 'I'm not lending you the compass.'

Mr Ford seems to choke. 'But it's mine!' he exclaims.

'No, it was Charlie's,' you tell him forcefully, 'and he gave it to me.'

'You haven't heard the last of this,' he splutters. 'And you can forget about that apprenticeship!' He turns on his heel and storms out.

Late that night, you stir in your sleep, then wake with a jolt. Something warm and large is next to your bed. It's scrabbling around your bedside table. You gasp and the figure turns to face you. It's Mr Ford.

For a moment, you stare at each other, wide-eyed in the moonlight. Then you scream. He claps a hot, heavy hand over your mouth. You fight to pull his hand away, but your arm is useless against his weight. You can't breathe. Finally he removes his hand, and you gulp in the air.

'I don't want to hurt you,' he growls. 'Where is it?'

You shake your head. You've hidden the compass

in the waistband of your undies – you can feel it pressing against your hip right now. You hear the *clip-clop* of an approaching nurse and Mr Ford escapes.

You consider following him but fall back against your pillows instead as the nurse's face appears above you. 'Just a bad dream,' you mumble. She offers you a sedative, but you refuse and lie awake, vigilant, for the rest of the night.

When Olenka visits you the next day, you tell her what happened and hand her the compass, which is warm from being pressed against your body all night. She promises to hide it. You were supposed to leave hospital that day, but you're so exhausted from being awake all night that the nurses insist on keeping you in for another day.

They find you out of bed in the middle of the second night, staring out the window. You can't tell them that you thought you saw the silhouette of Desmond Ford outside. They'll think you're going mad.

The following morning brings bad news. 'Olenka's house was broken into last night,' Mario tells you. 'What bad luck, hey?'

It's more than just bad luck. It's that damn Desmond Ford!

The nurses still won't let you out; they seem worried about you. You pace the corridors, desperate to see Olenka, feeling helpless and trapped. Olenka doesn't come.

That night, you dream that there are lumps under your skin. You try to push them down, but they force their way back to the surface, like hot marbles. Then they erupt. Smoke and lava ooze out in a black crackly coating. You're burning up.

You awake screaming, in a muck sweat. This time, the nurse doesn't let you refuse the sedative. 'You're being hysterical,' she says. 'You're waking everyone up.'

Around midday the next day you finally wake. The sedative must have been very strong. You stand and your legs threaten to buckle under you, but you're determined to find Desmond Ford. You make your way towards the door in your nightie, unsteady as a drunk on a ship.

'Get back to bed!' snaps the duty nurse, outraged. 'What are you doing?'

'It was Desmond Ford,' you try to tell her. 'He broke into Olenka's house! He has my compass!'

'What nonsense,' she says briskly. She forces you back into bed.

'They say you've been raving and staggering about,' says Mario that evening, concerned. 'What's going on? You were doing so well.'

'Get me out of here,' you implore him. 'Take me back to your place. Please, I'll explain everything.'

Mario places a hand on your head. 'You do feel hot,' he says. 'I hope it's not an infection.'

'I'm – not – sick!' you spit at him, then you feel your arm clamped, and the sting of something sharp.

'What is that?' you scream. 'Get it out!'

The nurse is attaching a drip. 'This will make you more comfortable, dear,' she soothes.

'No!' you cry. 'No!'

The nurse glances at Mario and he nods regretfully. 'It's for the best,' he says apologetically.

You try to fight back, but the nurse holds you down until you slide into a dreamy stupor.

There's someone in my room. He's trying to smother me. His whole weight is pressing into my body.

The nurses are here. They're force-feeding me biscuits. The biscuits are compasses.

Edik is here. He points a decomposing finger. 'It was her,' he says. 'It was her.'

You awake, gasping. You look at the needle

entering your arm. You try to rip it out with your teeth.

A nurse comes running. 'No!' she cries. 'Stop that!' She slaps your face, then adjusts the flow of whatever is coming through the drip. Cold sleep floods through you.

When you wake again, you can't move. You've been strapped down.

She tried to rip out her drip with her teeth.

She's refusing medicine.

She was out of bed staring out the window in the middle of the night.

She's disturbing the other patients.

Are those voices around your bed, or in your own head? All day long you are poked, prodded and sampled, as you slip in and out of clarity.

Her temperature is too high.

Is she having an allergic reaction to a drug?

Is it an infection?

She's paranoid. Hysterical. Hallucinating.

You're overwhelmed with anger. You try to punch or kick any nurses who touch you. They tighten the straps.

'I'm not crazy,' you tell Mario when he comes to visit that night. Your voice is slurred. Your tongue feels bloated.

'Well, no one would blame you if you were, after everything you've been through,' says Mario.

'But I'm not!' you insist. *I'm not, I'm not... am I?*

'Well, in that case, if you want them to believe that' – he nods towards a cluster of medical staff at the other end of the ward – 'you have to stop talking about Desmond Ford. He's a well-respected member of the community.'

'He's a bastard!'

'That may be, but if you keep saying he broke into Olenka's house and stole your compass, everyone will just think you're nuts. The authorities already blamed the robbery on the Aboriginal man who works in the kitchen.'

'No!' you shout. 'He didn't do it. It's not fair – those hateful bigots!' Then you start to cry, because you're trapped here and there's nothing you can do to help fix this. 'No...'

HOW MUCH TIME has passed? You're not in Cooma anymore. You kept fighting. Fighting to tell the truth... at least, what you thought was the truth. But you must have been mistaken. The compass reappeared on your bedside table and everyone said it had never disappeared in the first place.

You don't trust your own reality anymore. For example, just yesterday you thought you saw Charlie! Here, in this hospital, wherever it is. Canberra, you think. It's hard to get straight answers to even the simplest questions.

You don't trust anyone – not even Mario, who visits fortnightly. They are trying strange treatments to cure you of your madness: bitter medicines, electric shocks. You don't really care anymore. Your walk has become a shuffle, and the border between nightmare and reality has smudged.

'I'm cursed,' you tell the walls. 'Cursed, cursed.'

The walls just laugh.

THE END

✦ To return to your last choice and try again, go to page 207.

You feel your jaw harden as you look at Mr Ford. *This man lied to me*, you think. *He pretended Charlie was dead, and now that a fortune's at stake, he wants to change his tune. I don't trust him.*

'No way,' you say firmly, and you link your arm with Mario's. 'My loyalty lies with Charlie.' You try to march past Mr Ford.

'He won't recognise you!' he shouts, trying to intercept you. 'He forgets what he did yesterday! There's no point!'

'Mr Ford,' says Olenka firmly, stopping him in his tracks so you and Mario can get away, 'there is point.' She places an index finger on his chest. 'It is love.'

Mario points out his car. You jump into the passenger seat, and Mario revs the engine. This is a lot more action than you expected for your first day out of hospital in two months.

'There's a map in the glove box,' Mario tells you, and you roar out of Cooma, gravel spitting under the tyres. Your other feelings – excitement to be on a mission, and concern over what state you will find Charlie in – fade as you concentrate on the map.

'Oh no!' yells Mario. 'He's following us!' You crane your neck to look in the rear-vision mirror and see a grey jeep roaring up behind you, the grim face of Mr Ford behind the wheel.

'I'm going to pull over,' Mario shouts. 'This isn't safe!'

'Mario De Luca,' you scold him, 'are you Italian or not?'

He grins.

'And do you work as a tunneller a thousand metres underground or not? Risk is your middle name!'

'I know, but *you're* in the car...' he begins.

'I'm not made of china. Now go!' you command, and Mario accelerates. Mr Ford disappears in a cloud of dust. The road is steep and windy, and Mario is still speeding. You whoop and cheer. It feels like the car will take flight at each corner.

'Good God, he's keeping up!' cries Mario though, glancing in his rear-vision mirror again.

'Come on, give it all you've got!' you urge, feeling like a little kid on the swings. *Push me higher, Mamma!*

'I'm going as fast as I ca—' A bang like gunshot comes from underneath you. One of the tyres has burst. The car begins fishtailing down the road, and Mario struggles frantically to regain control. In slow motion, through the passenger window, you see the edge of the embankment coming closer and closer.

Mario swears as the left wheels of the car glide over the embankment and the car starts to tip. You fall against the window; Mario is thrown from his seat and lands against your right side. A constellation of glass bursts around you as the window smashes. Dirt is in your mouth and your ears. With a gigantic crunch, the car flips onto its roof and you are dropped on your head.

Then you are floating above the scene. A man leaps from a grey jeep and rushes to the smashed car. He struggles to right it, and you see him try to pull someone from the wreckage. You get a glimpse of dark curly hair: it's a girl.

You feel someone take your right hand. You turn and see a boy. After staring at him for an age, you realise he's someone you know.

Mario, you whisper.

The boy smiles.

THE END

✴ To return to your last choice and try again, go to page 216.

'I'll be honest with you, Mr Ford,' you tell him, 'I don't like you. I've never trusted you, and I still don't. But I want what's best for Charlie. I want to see him loved and cared for, in a home instead of a hospital. It's not too late for you to help with that.'

Mr Ford wipes his palms on his trousers. He nods. 'Thank you,' he says softly.

You, Mario and Mr Ford get into Mario's car and wave goodbye to Olenka. You're surprised to find that it feels like you're leaving home.

I belong here, you realise. *I want to stay.*

For a long time, the purr of the engine and rumble of the tyres are the only sounds. The shadows of trees and the sunlight between them flash across your face.

'I should warn you,' Mr Ford says eventually, 'that Charlie...won't be the Charlie you remember.' There's another long pause. You feel a sinking sadness. 'He looks much the same,' Mr Ford explains. 'But he has these things called flashbacks. He thinks the war is still going on around him. It's like a waking nightmare.'

'When we knew him,' you say, 'he didn't seem disturbed like that. What happened to him afterwards?'

'After he left the cave he tried to cross through German-occupied territory in Italy to rejoin the Allies,' says Mr Ford. 'The Nazis caught him, and he was treated mercilessly. He lived through things ... torture, really. He nearly died.'

'Poor Charlie,' says Mario.

'Yes, indeed,' says Mr Ford. 'After he came back, he couldn't trust anyone. He believed I was going to turn him over to the Germans. He accused me of poisoning his food, and hid strange letters written in code all over the house.'

'That must have been hard,' you say, beginning to understand why Mr Ford might have felt forced to put his brother into hospital.

He gives a deep sigh. 'Well, it was a lot harder for him. Still is. The doctors think that his trauma has prompted some sort of amnesia. One time when he still lived with me at home he nearly burnt the house down, because he forgot about the meal he was cooking – he went for a walk to the shops and got completely lost.'

You sit in silence for a while, feeling heavy-hearted. The war damaged so many lives. Not everyone can start again.

'I'm sorry I accused you of being a bad brother, Mr Ford,' you say. 'I didn't know the whole story.'

'That's all right,' Mr Ford says. 'You can call me Desmond, by the way. I really haven't done my best as a brother. I've thrown myself into my work and just tried to pretend he doesn't exist. I stopped visiting because it seemed to stir bad feelings up for both of us. After a while, it seemed easier to say he was dead.'

ONE OR TWO hours later, you arrive in Canberra – a tidy, new city with broad streets. Mario parks outside the hospital. Desmond leads the way, and you and Mario follow, holding hands.

You're nervous. *What will it be like in the psychiatric ward?*

You sign a visitor's form and tiptoe down the corridors, which smell of antiseptic. Some doors are open and you peer through them. There's a stubbly-faced man wearing a straitjacket to keep his arms pinioned across his body; a nurse is spoon-feeding him. In another room, a girl your age is rocking back and forth on her bed.

You feel queasy. 'I can't do this,' you tell Mario. 'I have to go outside. I can't see Charlie in here.'

'Charlie has to *live* here,' Mario reminds you. 'Come on, be brave. It's just a visit.'

You come to a door with 'Charlie Sanders' on it.

'It's Des,' Desmond calls out, knocking lightly. Then he opens the door.

The room inside has sage-green walls. Sitting on a white bed, in a bright square of sunlight, his arms wrapped around his knees, is Charlie. He's different – skinnier, more stooped. But he's still Charlie. A flood of relief washes away your horror. You want to run to him and squeeze him tight, but instead you wait as he slowly gets off the bed and comes to shake Desmond's hand.

Your heart is galloping. *Will he recognise me? Will he remember our time together?* He looks past his brother and meets your gaze. His blue eyes search your face.

'Charlie...' you whisper. 'Do you know who I am?'

You can hear his breathing, rapid and shaky. He lifts a trembling hand. His fingers brush against your cheek.

'You aren't real,' he stammers. 'I want you to be real – oh, you're so beautiful, just look how you've grown up! Oh,' he moans. 'I so want you to be real.' His eyes turn to Mario. 'Oh God, it's both of you! But older … and so strong …' He hasn't noticed your missing arm. 'Des, Des, Desmond,' Charlie stammers. 'I wish you could see these two. It's a good flashback – or a flash forward! I don't want them to go.'

'Charlie, we're real,' you assure him. 'Mario and I, we came to Australia. We're really here.'

'I can see them too, Charlie,' Desmond confirms. 'They're working with me at the Snowy.'

Charlie reaches out. Touches your cheek again. Folds you into a hug. Then he starts sobbing. 'I'm sorry you have to see me like this,' he chokes. His tears and breath feel humid on your shoulder. 'Sorry I left the cave. I put you in danger. When they tortured me, they wanted to know who hid me after I crashed. I never told them. At least, I don't think I did. But I have nightmares all the time. I feel like I did tell the Nazis where you were. I dream they tortured you, like they did me.'

'Charlie, we're all right,' you promise him. 'Look at me!' He lifts his head and surveys you and Mario again. When he sees your missing arm, he leaps backwards like a startled rabbit.

'They *did* catch you,' he breathes. 'It's my fault!' He squeezes his eyes shut and starts to hit his forehead with the heel of his hand.

'Charlie, no!' you cry. 'It's nothing to do with you. It was an accident at the Snowy.'

'She was being a hero,' Mario jokes gently. 'She hasn't changed since we hid you in the cat's guts.'

Charlie opens his eyes. A ghost of a smile flickers across his face. 'Really?' he asks, hardly daring to believe. 'No. This is all some crazy dream, it must be.'

'I'll prove it isn't,' says Desmond. He takes the golden compass from his pocket. The emerald shines in the sunlight. 'Hold this, Charlie. Feel it.'

A look of wonder comes over Charlie's face as he turns the compass back and forth in his hands. 'You were so angry with me when I said I gave this away.'

Desmond gives an embarrassed harrumph. 'I was hoping that would be one of the things you'd forgotten,' he mumbles.

'Our father's fortune…the code to the safe,' Charlie says, inspecting it. 'But the only markings on it are "C" and "D", just as I told you, for "Charlie" and "Desmond".'

'Not for "Charlie" and "Desmond",' you say. You still haven't told Desmond that you've cracked the code. 'I think the "C" is for "circumference", and the "D" is for "diameter".'

'I still don't get it,' Mario complains.

'The circumference is the distance around the

233

outside of a circle,' you explain to him again, patiently. 'The diameter is the measurement straight through the middle of a circle. If you divide a circle's circumference by its diameter, the answer is always pi. And that's—'

'Three point one four one!' cries Desmond.

'And so on and so on,' you explain. 'Three point one four one five nine two six five three five nine … the decimal places of pi's value go on forever. But you probably don't need all those numbers to unlock the safe.'

Charlie embraces you. 'You clever girl,' he murmurs. 'You wonderful person.'

'Well, you were my teacher,' you say, muffled by his hug. 'And it's still just a theory. Now we have to go and test it.'

YOU'RE TRYING TO get Charlie released from hospital, but the matron on duty at the reception desk is being obstinate. 'He has to be assessed by a doctor before I can let him go,' she insists.

'But it's for such a short while,' pleads Desmond. 'I'm his brother! And we're in a hurry!'

'Never mind,' says Charlie, defeated. 'I'll stay. You go.'

Having just spent two months in hospital yourself, you know how it can become your whole world; how you can no longer imagine a life beyond the walls. In Charlie's beaten, helpless air, you recognise yourself when you were at your lowest.

'We're getting you out of here,' you tell Charlie. 'This isn't a prison.'

'I'm authorised to restrain him at any time,' the matron says, getting to her feet.

'Can I help?' says an accented voice that sounds oddly familiar. You can only see a white-coated shoulder through a doorway behind the reception desk.

'Doctor Becker,' exclaims the matron, 'this patient is trying to—'

Becker, you think. *Isn't that…*

'Frieda!' you shout, and a blonde head pops through the doorway. It's her! Your heart swells and you feel butterflies in your stomach. Although it seems like a lifetime since you were on the boat together overthrowing the horrible Bob Dawe, she hasn't changed a bit. You laugh with joy.

She gasps in delight at the sight of you and runs to you for a hug, then stops short, aghast. *Oh, that's right*, you think, *my arm. I'm probably going to get this reaction a lot.*

'It "god orf",' you tell her in Lidia's Australian accent, nodding at the stump. 'But it's all right. I'll tell you about it later. Can you get us out of here?'

Frieda's smile returns. 'I'll do my best,' she says.

THREE ... ONE ...

The dial on the safe clicks as you rotate it into each position. You're kneeling on the cool concrete floor of the safe deposits room in the back of the Canberra bank. Every slight noise echoes – you're sure you can hear your heart beating.

Mario, Desmond and Charlie lean over you, watching and waiting. The ghost of old Mr Ford Senior is probably watching you too.

Desmond thinks the safe might contain a fortune in banknotes. Charlie hopes there'll be some of his mother's jewellery.

'If only the deeds to Sandford's Rise were in there,' muses Charlie now. 'But the family farm is gone.'

'I didn't want to sell it,' says Desmond. 'We were nearly broke. I couldn't manage it alone. Bob Dawe seemed to think he might find gold there – he gave me a good price.'

'I know,' sighs Charlie. 'But I miss it so much.'

'Me too,' agrees Desmond. 'Me too.'

Four … one …

With a spring-loaded *pop*, the door to the safe swings open. It is nearly empty inside, except for a few large square leather-bound books. You move back and let Charlie reach in to take them.

'Photo albums,' he breathes. The pages creak slightly as he turns them.

'That's it?' Mario exclaims. 'Shake them – maybe money will fall out, or a treasure map!'

'No, Mario,' says Charlie. He sits cross-legged on the floor, and Desmond sits beside him. 'This is the treasure.' He turns to his brother. Desmond's face is awash with confusion. 'Des, you don't still have the letter, do you? From Dad?'

Des rummages in his pocket. 'Yes, I brought it with me. There's a bit where he talks about the treasure … ah, this is it.' And he starts to read:

Of course the farm means a lot to me, being my life's work. But there is a greater treasure by far, a forgotten treasure – my last and best legacy. It's in a safe at my bank in Canberra. Charlie has the code: it was engraved on his mother's compass, which he took to the war. Charlie, I know you haven't been well lately …

Desmond breaks off, choking up. He hands the letter to Charlie, who keeps reading.

Charlie, I know you haven't been well lately. You've been forgetting things, imagining things, and Des, you've been struggling with it. You were always such different personalities, and maybe I didn't do enough to bring you together. But it's my dying wish that you two will open this safe together and recover the treasure inside. And you know that if you don't honour your old man's dying wish, I'll return to haunt you from beyond the grave! Ha, ha, ha.

Seriously, though, don't lose each other. Don't forget me. Or your mother. Although you've both had to be strong to survive, I know you both have kind hearts, and I hope you'll hold me there in your hearts always.

Your loving dad

Desmond sobs quietly and Charlie holds him. Mario takes your hand.

'That was his last act,' Desmond says. 'He wanted to bring us back together, to appreciate what we had – our family. And all along, I thought it was gold or a stash of money. After Dad died, when

I asked Charlie about the compass and found out Charlie had given it away, I was furious. I did the opposite of what Dad wanted.'

'It's all right,' says Charlie. You notice as he comforts his brother that there's a steadiness to him and a clarity he didn't have at the hospital. 'I think this is all turning out exactly how it was meant to. Let's go, so we can look at the pictures together.'

You walk outside into the sunlight and find a bench under some trees on the street.

'You look like mini-copies of your current selves,' laughs Mario, looking at the photos, and he's right: young Charlie was fair and slim, just like he is now, and Desmond was always dark and sturdy. There they are climbing a tree...covered in mud from the dam...feeding an orphaned calf from a bottle...struggling together to lift an enormous pumpkin. The only thing matching is their grins.

'We had fun, didn't we?' Charlie says. 'Before boarding school...'

There's a willowy, gentle-looking woman in some of the photos – their mother. Their father was a stocky man, his face in the pictures always shaded by the brim of his ancient-looking hat.

'She was a Sanders and he was a Ford,' Charlie explains to you. 'She kept her maiden name after marriage and gave it to me, too. All the local families thought that was very odd. "Sandford's Rise" is a combination of their two names. They changed the name of the farm when they married, but it was Mum's family's property originally. I think it used to be called "Shadow's Rest". No one knows why.'

There's another album with black-and-white photos dating back to the late eighteen hundreds. 'There are Mum's ancestors,' says Desmond. 'The bloke on the left with the eye-patch was her great-great-grandpa.' You look closely at the two men with their arms around each other, their faces sombre.

'They're twins!' you exclaim.

'That's right,' says Desmond. 'They made their fortune on the goldfields, I believe, then the one with the eye-patch bought Sandford's Rise – or Shadow's Rest, as he named it. The compass used to be his; he's holding it in that photo.' You look closely and see that he's right.

That reminds you of something: the cornetto. It was in your family for at least as long as the compass was in Charlie's, and during the war, thanks to you and Charlie, those two golden heirlooms swapped places. Did it really cause all that bad luck? You don't think so anymore. But now that the compass is back with Charlie, it's time for the cornetto to come back to you – if Charlie still has it.

'Do you remember the cornetto I gave you – the golden charm?' you ask.

Charlie's face falls. 'They wouldn't let me keep it in the hospital. I wore it every day until then.'

'I know where it is,' Des says. He walks over to Mario's parked car, opens the boot, and returns with a leather satchel. 'Doctor Becker gave me this as we were leaving the hospital – it's what you had with you when you were admitted. All yours, Charlie.'

Charlie draws a notebook, a pen and a well-worn cardigan from the bag, then finally a chain of gold. He pours it into your palm. It seems to tingle as it touches your skin. *It's so small*, you think. *Just a trinket, really. But in a way, it helped cause all this.*

Mario picks up the notebook and leafs through it. It's full of Charlie's pencil sketches. 'There's Lenola!' he gasps. 'And there's me!' You crane your neck to look too. They're amazingly lifelike.

'I drew all these from memory,' Charlie says proudly. 'But … my memories of those days weren't all good.' As the pages go on, the drawings become more jagged, the shadows more menacing. There's another picture of you and Mario, but you can hardly see it because Charlie has written over the top, again and again, *keep them safe keep them safe keep them safe.* There's another picture of Cat's Mouth filled with German soldiers, their figures deeply etched in black as if Charlie were trying to carve them out of the paper with his pencil. Laced over the top, in clouds of letters, he's written *don't tell don't tell don't tell.*

'I can't look at this,' says Charlie. He's started to tremble.

'Is a flashback coming?' you ask.

'Maybe.' Charlie suddenly stands up, runs to Mario's car and locks himself inside. You can see him through the windows, curled up on the passenger seat. His eyes are wide and terrified – he seems to be breathing very fast. When Mario tries to unlock the door and open it, Charlie holds tightly to the door and shakes his head. So you stand by the car for fifteen minutes, occasionally calling out, 'Are you okay, Charlie?'

'I'm okay,' you hear him reply.

'Can I help?'

'No.'

Eventually, he comes out. 'It feels like you're having a heart attack,' he says in a shaky voice. 'The memories start playing like a film, and all you can do is watch.'

'It must be horrible,' you say. You hug him. He's sweaty, as though he's run a marathon.

CHARLIE GOES BACK to the hospital that afternoon without protest. 'I know I can't live alone just yet,' he says. 'But it would be nice to get out more.'

'We'll be down every weekend,' says Mario. 'Just try to stop us!'

'Oh,' you gasp, 'Desmond, the apprenticeship contract you offered me – I ripped it in half this morning! Before I realised how everything would turn out!'

Desmond just laughs. 'You'll have to try harder than that to get out of working for me,' he said, and your heart fills with gladness and relief. You are going to be an engineer – for real! Charlie and Mario are beaming too.

Frieda's shift has just ended, and she takes you for a cup of tea in the staffroom, while Mario and Desmond go for a beer. Seeing her is special, in a way you can't quite put words to. The two of you talk and talk.

'And you'll never believe it,' you conclude. 'Desmond sold the family farm, Sandford's Rise, to our old friend, Bob Dawe!'

'You're joking!' she cries. 'Bob Dawe – what a scheming crook he was. You know, what he did on the boat was just small change for him. He'd been laundering money for international criminal gangs, robbing people blind, and it's finally caught up with him. He's going to trial at last, in Sydney, and I'm going to be a witness!'

'You're going to tell everyone what he did?' you ask. 'You're a hero! Wow, I wish I could be there in court when he gets his comeuppance!'

'You should come,' says Frieda, her eyes twinkling. 'As my moral support.'

SO YOU DO. Frieda holds her head high on the witness stand and commands the jury's attention. You want to leap to your feet and cheer when she's done, but just give her a wink and a grin.

It's weird to see Bob Dawe again. He seemed so threatening and powerful on the boat. Now he just looks like a toad with indigestion. He notices you in the gallery. Then he notices your arm. You meet his gaze, and stare him down. He's so unnerved that he stumbles over his answer and has to ask the prosecutor to repeat the question. You smile and hold your head high, like Frieda.

The jury adjourns, and you and Frieda get pastries for lunch in downtown Sydney. At last the jury returns, the judge raps his gavel, and the foreman of the jury stands up and presents their verdict.

'Guilty, Your Honour.'

Frieda squeezes your hand and you get a happy, fizzy-soda feeling in your body.

'Mister Robert Dawe,' intones the judge, 'you have been found guilty on five counts of fraud and two counts of embezzlement. Your lawyer has indicated that you have declared bankruptcy and your assets will be liquidated. However, I do not believe this to be enough of a punishment, so I hereby sentence you to ten years' gaol without parole.'

The judge's convoluted English is hard to follow, but you caught *ten years' gaol* well enough. 'What does *your assets will be liquidated* mean?' you ask Frieda, when you get outside on the street. 'It sounds like they're going to chop off his head and put it through a mincer!'

She snorts with laughter. 'It just means that everything he owns will be sold and the money will be used to pay off his debts.'

You mentally add *liquidate assets* to your English vocabulary. Then you suddenly realise what that means. 'Frieda!' you cry. 'He'll have to sell Sandford's Rise! Charlie and Des can buy it back!' You fish the cornetto out of your pocket and swing it around over your head. The gold twinkles in the sunshine. 'The good luck is back!' you cry. A few people turn to stare, and Frieda starts laughing.

'By the end of our boat ride, you thought your mother was crazy for believing in that curse,' she says. 'But now you believe in it again too?'

'Of course not.' You laugh. 'But having said that, it's not just a piece of gold, either. This necklace has a story as old as my family. I crossed the world to find it. It ties me to Charlie, and to my home. It's a part of so many memories.'

Freida gives you a giant hug. Just then, you catch sight of someone over her shoulder. He's sitting against the wall of a building, with his cap laid out upside down on the ground in front of him. He's dark-skinned, and he doesn't lift his eyes from the pavement. A cardboard sign in front of him reads: 'I FOUGHT IN WW2 TO SAVE AUSTRALIA. NOW I CAN'T GET VETERAN'S HOUSING. PLEASE HELP.'

Your heart goes out to this man. Why can't he get veteran's housing? People on the street just walk by and ignore him. If ever a man deserved good fortune, you decide, it's this man. He fought for your freedom in the war, and now you're a free woman in his country.

The cornetto is still in your hand. A thought occurs to you: *I could give him this.* Mamma would wring your neck if she knew, of course. She'll always believe in the curse, and maybe she'll only feel right once she has the cornetto back. But you don't want it to have such a hold over her. You want Mamma to start making her own luck, like you've made yours.

In your heart, you can't bear to give the cornetto away. It means too much to everyone. But your brain argues that's precisely the reason you should give it away – to prove the idea of the curse doesn't mean anything anymore, and to help someone who might need it more than you do.

✳ If you decide to keep the cornetto to send back to Mamma, go to page 247.

✳ If you decide to give the cornetto to the man with the sign, go to page 250.

You drop the cornetto into your pocket and bring some coins out instead. The man looks up, squinting against the sunlight as you approach him.

'Thank you for your service,' you say, dropping the coins in his hat.

He nods.

'I almost decided to give the cornetto to that man, but I've decided Mamma needs it more,' you say to Frieda as you fall back into step beside her.

Frieda laughs again. 'You know that if you give that cornetto back to your mother, you're just participating in her delusion,' she chides you gently.

'I know,' you say, 'but Mamma believes it, and if she thinks the curse is gone, it will change her whole life. She'll feel free again, and that's something real.'

You catch the afternoon train home to Cooma, and head straight to the post office to write Mamma a letter. You beam as you imagine the expression on her face when she opens it.

Dear Mamma,

There's something I have to tell you. After a terrible accident in the Snowy Mountains, I lost my arm. I was trying to save the life of my friend Edik, but he didn't make it. I know you'll think this is bad luck, Mamma, but the amazingly good luck is that I survived.

I finally found Charlie in a hospital in Canberra, and he gave me back our family cornetto. I'm sorry I ever stole it, Mamma. I hope that by finally holding it again, you can feel at peace. I've found that peace myself, through enduring worse times than I ever thought possible.

Life is precious, Mamma. I've forged my own way in this amazing land, and made so many friends. Mario is the best of them all. They are all going to help me learn to live with one arm. Edik's wife, Olenka, will need help to live without her husband, and Charlie will need help to live outside the hospital. But we will all be okay, because we all have each other.

Maybe one day you'll come and join us here. That would make me so happy. Charlie's farm is called Sandford's Rise, and I'm longing to see it.

You lift the golden cornetto to your lips and lightly kiss it. Then you wrap it tightly in a sheet of paper, and seal it inside the envelope with Mamma's name and address on the front. You hear the flutter of the envelope as it lands among the others.

Your new job starts on Monday: apprentice engineer for the Snowy Mountains Hydro Electric Authority. You can hardly wait.

✴ Go to page 252.

You walk over to the beggar and he squints against the sunlight as he looks up at you.

'Thank you for fighting for our country,' you say.

He doesn't reply, just nods.

'This is an old Italian good-luck charm,' you tell him, crouching down and showing him the cornetto. 'You don't have to keep it – you can sell it, if you'd rather have the money. But I hope it does you some good.'

You tip it into his palm. It feels like a current of energy pouring out. The man takes it from his palm and inspects it closely.

'This is from Italy, where you're from?' he asks.

'Yes, it's been in my family a long time.'

He nods slowly. Then he smiles. 'This means more than money,' he says. 'My people have been here forever and you're welcome here, sister. Don't listen to anyone who tells you you're not.'

He offers his left hand for you to shake – he's noticed you won't be able to do a right-handed shake, and without saying a word, he's just shown you a kindness in return.

As you walk away, smiling, your heart swells so much that it feels as if it's actually trying to grow larger inside your chest.

'Well, there goes the cornetto,' you say to Frieda. 'Off into the world again.'

It's the second time you've given it away. But this time, you know what you're doing. You feel a lightness – a freedom. Whatever comes your way in the future, you know that you can handle it.

'Good on you.' Frieda smiles. 'But what is your poor old mamma going to say?'

'Well...' You laugh. 'She'll probably want to kill me with her bare hands. But she'll have to cross the world to do that, and by the time she gets here, she might have managed to turn her bad luck upside down all by herself, like I did.'

Maybe moving here would be just what she needs, you think. *A fresh start. I'll have to see if I can convince her. Imagine if the whole family could come!*

'Let's make sure you don't miss your train now, Miss Apprentice Engineer,' jokes Frieda. 'That really would be bad luck!'

Your new job begins on Monday. You can't wait to begin. You can't wait to get home.

✦ Go to page 252.

'Passa … the … salta,' says Mamma.

'Zia,' laughs Mario, 'it's just "pass the salt". Even when you try to speak English, it sounds like Italian!'

'Naughty boy, rude boy!' she exclaims in English, wagging her finger at him, but she's laughing. 'You teacha your children speaka bad to they nonna.'

'Lidia, Teodoro,' Mario says to them, 'you must always be kind to Nonna. *Never* call her walrus-breath … or cabbage-toes … or a sausage-nosed old teabag …'

'What are you calling me?' she cries in Italian.

'Never call her … a rotten apple!' laughs Lidia in English.

'Or a cow-pat!' cries Teodor, nearly falling off his chair.

'I'll teach them what to call their daddy in Italian if you don't behave,' Mamma chuckles to Mario, still speaking Italian. 'I know all of *those* words!'

Olenka comes into the dining room, one hand resting on her big, round belly. She kisses Mario on the lips and eases herself into the chair next to him.

'You're getting our children all worked up,' she scolds him, but she's smiling.

Mario takes her hand. 'But that's why you love me,' he protests. 'Mischief-maker Number One.'

Desmond taps his beer glass with a fork, calling for hush. 'Now, you all know what the occasion is today,' he announces. 'It's five years since we finally got our home back.'

You look at the faces around the table. There's Mamma and your three siblings, Giulia, Tommaso and Alessandro, whom you still can't believe is a teenager already. Then there's Mario, Charlie, Frieda, Desmond, Olenka and her two – soon to be three – children. Your beautiful patchwork family.

'We've all come further than I ever hoped,' Desmond continues. 'I don't know if it was luck that brought us together, or fate—'

'I think it was love!' calls out Frieda. You feel a blush run to your face as her sparkling eyes catch yours. Frieda makes you so happy – every moment with her is golden. It's an incredible, precious gift that she seems to feel the same way about you.

It's almost too good to be true, you think. *Our family all together… my promotion at Snowy. We really have found our fortune.*

'Well, whatever brought us here,' finishes Des, 'this is now our home. And it will be home to the next generation to come, too. To Sandford's Rise!' he calls, raising his glass.

'To Sandford's Rise!' everyone choruses.

You sip your drink and then chuckle to yourself about a memory from long ago.

'What are you laughing about?' Charlie asks you.

'That letter Mario sent – the fake one from you, that invited him to work here. It was a complete lie, yet here we are on this very farm; it came true after all,' you muse. There's a contented pause around the table. Then you remember something. 'I've never asked you, Mario – why did you put that code in there? Was it meant to tease me?'

'What are you talking about?' asks Mario, puzzled.

You remember the letter off by heart, so you scribble it onto a scrap of paper. 'If you leave off the "Dear Mario" at the start, then circle every seventh word, it makes a message, see?' you tell him. You worked this out a year or so ago, but never got around to asking Mario about it.

As you write it down now, everyone crowds around to look.

Dear Mario,
I hope that this letter has FOUND
you well. It was my great FORTUNE
to be rescued by you and HIDDEN.
This letter is to invite you ON
a voyage to Australia, to my FARM
to work there. If you can COME,
I'd be delighted to see you AND
you would be very welcome to SHARE
my home and food, such as IT
is. Best wishes to one and ALL,
Charlie

'It says, "Found fortune hidden on farm, come and share it all",' you point out. Mario's jaw has dropped.

'I did *not* put that in there,' he insists, stunned. 'That's ... just weird.'

'Patterns.' Frieda smiles. 'The human brain is wired to find them everywhere.'

'But even you have to admit, that's a pretty big coincidence,' you argue.

When Mario explains to Mamma what's going on, she gets wildly excited and jumps from her chair. 'It's a sign!' she crows in Italian. 'This farm will make you all rich! Oh, thank you, Jesus, Mary and Joseph!'

'Well, Bob Dawe did think he was going to strike gold here,' says Desmond. 'All the geological signs pointed to it, apparently.'

'Imagine mining machines pulling apart Sandford's Rise,' says Charlie sadly. 'I'm glad it never happened. But I used to find little specks of it in the stream when I was a boy. Lidia and Teodor, after lunch, I'll take you panning for gold, all right?'

The kids jump and cheer.

'Do you think you're lucky?' Frieda teases the children.

'I know we are,' you tell her. 'All of us.'

THE END

FACT FILE:

WOMEN IN WORLD WAR II

World War II lasted from 1939 to 1945. It involved most countries in the world, who broadly formed into two sides: the Allies (including Australia, Britain, France, the Soviet Union and the USA) and the Axis (including Germany, Italy – at first – and Japan). Seventy to eighty-five million people were killed, and it remains the deadliest conflict in human history to this day.

This book begins in Italy in 1943. Italy fought alongside the Axis powers but changed sides in the war and joined the Allies in October 1943. Then the Allies fought alongside Italian resistance groups to drive the occupying German forces out of Italy. (Some Italian soldiers in the north, however, were forced to keep fighting alongside the Germans as 'military internees'.)

Before the war, very few women were in the workforce – instead, they were expected to stay at home full-time, doing housework and raising children while the men went to work. In Australia, Britain and the USA during World War II, however, women were able to become medics, drivers, mechanics and even spies, although they weren't allowed to fight the enemy face-to-face. Nancy Wake, a New Zealander, was a famous spy from this time. She was so sneaky that the Gestapo (German secret police) nicknamed her 'the White Mouse', because they could never catch her!

One country that did allow women to fight in World War II was Russia. Their snipers included women such as Klavdiya Kalugina, who joined up when she was only seventeen, and Lyudmila Pavlichenko, a commander who killed 309 soldiers, making her one of the deadliest military snipers in history.

Over the last few decades, women have taken on more defence force roles, working as submarine captains, air force squadron leaders and more. In 2016, Australia finally allowed women into frontline combat roles.

Would you want to fight on the front line if your country was invaded? Or is there another role you think you'd be better at, like being a spy, a navigator, or a doctor? People of all genders can be heroes, and not just because they're the strongest or the fittest – true bravery comes from within.

✦ Return to page 27 to make your choice.

FACT FILE:

EUROPEAN MIGRATION AFTER WORLD WAR II

World War II triggered the greatest global migration ever seen at that time in human history (although we have since surpassed it). Many people had lost their families and homes in the war.

This was especially so for Jewish people, who had suffered horrifically as Hitler and his Nazis attempted genocide (the murder of an entire race or nation of people) against them. Other refugees within Europe were trying to escape Communist states that were created at the end of World War II and were controlled by the Soviet Union. Everyone despaired at the lack of food, shelter and other necessities after the war.

New workers were needed all around the world to help boost countries' economies and workforces. Immigration officials from Australia travelled to Europe to advertise Australia as a land of exciting new opportunities.

The voyage from Italy to Australia by boat

took six to eight weeks, and once immigrants arrived they had to deal with the shock of a very unfamiliar culture and language. Italian migrants were unable to find even simple ingredients they were accustomed to using in their cooking, like garlic or olive oil, and many racist Anglo-Celtic Australians mistrusted these 'foreigners'.

Letters and news took weeks to travel back and forth between continents, and immigrants knew they might never again see the family and friends they had left behind. Despite the risks and hardships European migrants endured, the journeys that they took after World War II have made the world richer in many different ways.

◇━◈━◇────◇━◈━◇

✦ Return to page 56 to make your choice.

FACT FILE:
THE WHITE AUSTRALIA POLICY

The Australian colonies federated in 1901. Horribly, the very first act of the new Federal Parliament was the *Immigration Restriction Act*, which was designed to exclude migrants whom the government considered unacceptable – usually those who weren't British or from certain white countries in Europe. This was one of many laws throughout Australia's history that amounted to a 'White Australia Policy'.

Supporters of the White Australia Policy wrongly thought that Australia would be more harmonious and better off if only white people were allowed to move there. These supporters completely ignored the fact that Australia had been a nation of black Aboriginal and Torres Strait Islander people for tens of thousands of years before white colonisers stole the land.

After World War II, the White Australia Policy was relaxed somewhat to allow Southern Europeans such as Italians and Greeks to move there, although the government still restricted those from many other countries. Over the following decades, the White Australia Policy was slowly reversed, until at last, only in 1975, the Whitlam Labor government made it unlawful to discriminate against anybody based on their 'race'.

Now, we look back on the White Australia Policy with shame. The laws were not only racist and hurtful to those they discriminated against; they also meant that for many decades Australia missed out on the cultural richness and the many things Australians could have learnt by welcoming a diversity of people.

Australia is now declared to be one of the most successful multicultural nations in the world, although our problems with racism are far from over. There are, disgracefully, still groups in Australia - with representatives in parliament - who call for a return of the White Australia Policy. Aboriginal and Torres Strait Islander peoples are often not treated with the respect that they should be. And sensationalist and racist publications similar to *Truth* (a real newspaper from Sydney, 1890-1958, and Melbourne, 1902-1995, featured in this book) still exist today and try to falsely represent non-white groups of people in a negative light.

Have your wits about you when you read the news! Is it really the *Truth*?

✦ Return to page 108 to continue with the story.

FACT FILE:

THE SNOWY SCHEME

There are many ways that electricity can be created, for example by solar panels, or by turbines (big wheels) turned by wind, water or steam. Some of these methods are more harmful to the environment than others, but what they all have in common (except solar panels) is that they create electricity by powering turbines that spin huge magnets inside a wire coil to create an electric current.

Hydro-electric power is created by using water to turn the turbines, just as people used to use water to drive their mills or waterwheels centuries ago. Creating a hydro-electric scheme means drastically altering the landscape by damming rivers, and diverting the water down steep pipes. This can have a huge impact on the environment, although modern dams are doing a better job than the old ones at mimicking natural ecosystem flows and habitats. However, once a hydro-electric scheme is up and running, the power it generates is renewable and free from pollution.

In the 1950s, when this book is set, the Snowy Mountains Hydro Electric Scheme ('the Snowy' for short) was one of the most ambitious engineering projects in the world. It took twenty-five years to complete and 100,000 people from over thirty countries worked on it.

Around two-thirds of Snowy workers were migrants who had left the horrors of World War II behind to start a new life. At first, Snowy bosses worried that mixing together workers of different nationalities who had been at war with each other would lead to fights. But people had had enough of fighting: they were keen to put their pasts behind them and work on a new, exciting project.

Often the work was very hard physical labour, in remote wild areas or deep underground. Safety regulations were less strict in those days than they are now, and the technology was more basic. There were accidents, some of which were fatal: one hundred and twenty-one people died during the construction of the Snowy Scheme.

The Snowy Scheme is still in operation and remains one of the most complex and impressive civil-engineering projects in the world. These days, it has extremely high standards for workplace safety and also actively recruits women into senior and technical positions. The existing scheme links seven power stations and sixteen dams with one hundred and forty-five kilometres of tunnels and eighty kilometres of aqueducts.

◇━◇━━━◇━◇

✴ Return to page 133 to make your choice.

FACT FILE:
WOMEN'S RIGHTS

Although you, dear reader, were hopefully raised to see women and men as equal, the truth is that for most of recorded human history, things haven't been seen this way, and often still aren't. Throughout history, women have been controlled, criticised and ordered about by men. Institutions such as governments, religions and businesses have been set up mostly to benefit men.

All over the world, women and girls still experience violence and discrimination because of their gender. In 1950s Australia, where this book is set, women faced a tough battle to be recognised as equal to men. Generally, at that time, society believed that a woman's most important job was to marry, have children, and keep her husband happy by cooking perfect meals, caring for the children, and keeping the house sparkling clean and beautiful. (Does that sound boring to you? It was to a lot of women then, as well!) Only one in five university students was female, and women who wanted an education or a career (especially in a male-dominated field like engineering) would have been treated with scorn.

Now, women can become pastors and priests, join the army, marry and divorce as they wish, and take maternity leave without losing their jobs – none of which they could legally do in the 1950s. Thanks to the efforts of those who campaigned for women's rights and led the way, women have more opportunities than ever before.

However, we still have some way to go to achieving true equality. The Human Rights Commission reports that, as of 2018, women spend twice as many hours a day as men doing unpaid domestic work. They are three times more likely to be the victims of domestic violence than men, and they still only earn eighty-five cents for every dollar a man makes. In Indigenous communities in Australia and other countries, particularly countries affected by war or poverty, those statistics are much worse. In sexist societies, men are harmed too, because they are pressured into being tough, competitive and aggressive all the time.

True gender equality starts in our own communities. Do you ever see sexist things in your school playground, such as girls being told not to join in a rough sports game, or boys being teased for crying? Do you ever notice at a family gathering that the mothers, aunties and grandmas are doing more housework than the fathers, uncles and grandpas?

If you notice these things, take a stand, by stepping in and saying you don't think it's right! Everyone deserves equal rights, and equal responsibilities.

✳ Return to page 133 to make your choice.

FACT FILE:

MENTAL HEALTH AND TREATMENT

We all feel a wide range of emotions, such as anger, joy, sadness and fear. Sometimes we can swing between emotions very quickly, and sometimes our feelings can frighten us, or those around us. Sometimes we can think or believe things that aren't true, such as that our friends secretly hate us, or that it was our fault that our parents got a divorce. Sometimes we get overwhelmed or confused about how to handle strong feelings, and this can interfere with normal life. Almost everyone feels like this from time to time. It's good to get help with those strong feelings, but experiencing them doesn't mean you have a mental illness.

Nobody thinks it's normal to be happy all the time, or that we even should be. We're actually lucky that we can experience a wide range of emotions, because we need all our feelings to be able to understand the world and form healthy relationships. But sometimes a person can really struggle to get back to a balanced state of mind. Their strong feelings or disturbed thoughts can seem to dominate every part of their life, and they can struggle to live normally. They might be classified by a doctor as having a mental illness, such as depression or anxiety (both of which are very common and affect one and two million Australians respectively).

Luckily, our understanding of mental illness has come a long way in the past centuries. It is no longer thought of, as it once was long ago, as being caused by demons, and those who are mentally ill are no longer locked away in asylums in horrific conditions. Throughout history, doctors have tried strange and sometimes damaging therapies to try to 'cure' mental illness, such as lobotomies (surgery to remove parts of the brain), experimental medicines, and inducing hypothermia through extreme cold. Overall, it is only recently that society has begun to treat people with mental health conditions with kindness and respect.

In the 1950s, when this book is set, it was still taboo to admit that you, or a family member, had a mental illness, and you could still be subjected to many of the experimental and damaging treatments mentioned above.

Veterans like Charlie who came back from World War II with what we would now call Post Traumatic Stress Disorder (PTSD) often buried their feelings and never talked about the terrible things they had seen. Pretending that mental health problems don't exist only makes them worse.

These days, doctors and mental health advocates encourage everyone to talk about the stresses and strong feelings in our lives, so that we can get support before they turn into major, harmful problems. Sometimes certain drugs can be used to help patients concentrate, relax, or feel more cheerful or calm again. A wide range of other therapies including art therapy, play therapy and family counselling can also help.

If you or anyone you know is under emotional stress, talk to a trusted adult, or call a counselling helpline. In Australia, you can call Kids Helpline on 1800 55 1800.

✳ Return to page 216 to make your choice.

DID THAT
REALLY HAPPEN?

World War II Allied pilots hidden in caves in Lenola, Italy...

YES, BUT THEY WERE AMERICANS. I was originally told a second-hand family story that a distant relation of mine, Dan Quinto, had helped to hide an Australian pilot in the caves around Lenola, and kept him alive for eight months until the war ended. The story went that when the war was over, this Australian pilot invited Dan to come and work on his family's property, and that was how the Quintos' life in Australia had begun. When I traced the story back to Dan, he said that no, actually, there were three men rescued from the crashed plane, they were all American, and although his family did hide them in caves and risk their lives to save them from the Germans for eight months, after the war they had no further contact with them. Dan's family came to Australia because a wealthy landowner wanted to recruit labourers for land-clearing. But the second-hand story was so satisfying that it had already claimed its place in my heart, and in this book! It does, however, create a historical inaccuracy: the Australian Air Force *was* involved in the Allied invasion of southern Italy generally, but not of Lenola.

Ships' captains withholding rations to sell for profit...

YES, ACCORDING TO THE LEGENDS OF ANTONIO. Antonio Pani, an ex-Snowy Scheme employee, told me that this did indeed happen on his boat journey to Australia. Once the source of the food shortage was revealed, he and some friends apparently mutinied, locking the ship's captain in a cupboard! When they reached Australia they were at first arrested, then released when they told their story. Toni was among many colourful raconteurs whom I met while researching this book.

Accidents on the Snowy Scheme...

YES, BUT I'VE ALTERED NAMES AND CIRCUMSTANCES IN THIS STORY. Most people I talked to about their time on the Snowy Scheme could remember witnessing an accident or at least hearing about one, and many could remember work that was so intense and dangerous it's lucky they survived. Wally Stumpf told me about a man hiding under a skip who lost an arm when a metal pipe slipped out of its sling and came hurtling down the tunnel. Nick Barlee told me about the accidental explosions that occurred underground when tunnellers drilled into old holes with traces of explosive left behind. Frank Rodwell told me of the people who died of asphyxiation after leaving a kerosene heater on overnight, and he also told me of the unforgettable 'staring man' who emptied his food onto the tabletop in the mess hall every night. These events occurred to different people in different years than the ones mentioned here, but they all happened. So did many other incredible tales, which couldn't all fit into this book.

Aboriginal and Torres Strait Islander veterans being denied a fair go...

SADLY, THIS IS TRUE. Towards the end of this book, 'you' see a dark-skinned war veteran on the streets of Sydney. He is a returned Indigenous soldier. During World War II, many Indigenous people went to war for Australia, even though Australia still discriminated against them terribly. Would you go to war for a country that didn't even give your peoples the right to vote? How would you feel about fighting for a government that still had the policy of stealing your children away from their families? These heroic soldiers put their lives on the line and stood up to defend a nation whose governments since colonisation had never defended them. If they hoped their service might change things when they came home, they were sadly mistaken. Many Indigenous ex-servicemen were denied entry into RSL groups, had their veteran's pensions withheld, and were excluded from Legacy funding. All Indigenous returned soldiers had to face the injustice of being treated as less than equals in a country they had made enormous sacrifices to defend. In 2017, Indigenous veterans were invited to lead the ANZAC Day marches for the first time.

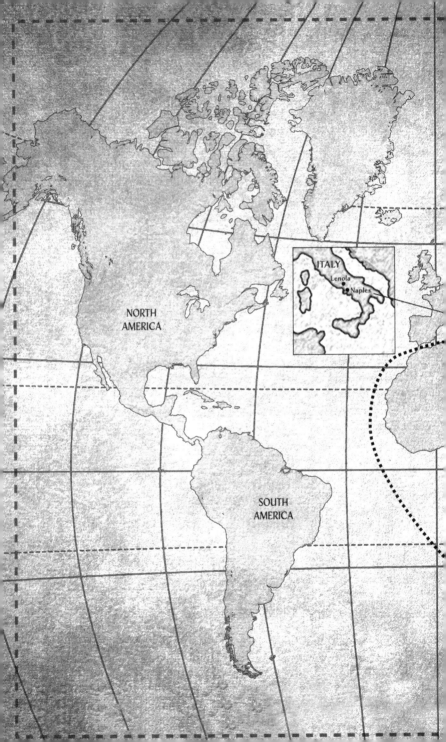

ACKNOWLEDGEMENTS

SO MANY PEOPLE shared their wonderful stories with me while I researched this book. Thank you to my Zia Rosella and Dan and Joe Quinto, for tales of the airman over Lenola – I hope you are happy to see this story take flight into imagination. My deepest thanks to you also, Zia Rosella, for all your advice on the book's Italian cultural content and your endless generosity and patience.

I was lucky to be given a grant by Snowy Mountains Hydro to travel to Canberra, Cooma and Cabramurra and see these places for myself. Thank you to Snowy Mountains Hydro, and to all the people who contributed to this research trip, particularly Lara Sav from Snowy Hydro, Sandy Van Der Toorn at Woden Community Service, and my cousin Jenni Savigny in Canberra, who just happened to be working on an oral histories project with ex-Snowy workers at the same time!

I was also incredibly lucky to interview many

people who still remember World War II, and who were among the first migrants to arrive in Australia after the war and begin work on the Snowy Hydro Scheme. A huge thank you goes to all the Snowy workers who shared their stories with me in interviews: Antonio Pani; Walter and Marian Stumpf; Bill Benson; Artur Baumhammer; Carlo Aggio; Frank Rodwell; Jock Montgomery; Norm Kopievsky; Ervino Bertolin; Bruno Bruno; and next generation Snowy worker Nick Barlee. It's amazing to think that this extraordinary time in history all happened within your lifetimes.

Thanks to everyone who helped with consultation when I wrote my way into sensitive ground: Dr Jared Thomas for advising me on the Indigenous content; Amelia Padgett, Josh Santospirito and Alice Downie for their advice on the sections involving mental illness; Rachel Markos for her perspective on what the word 'wog' means for Greek Australians today; and all the Polish friends-of-friends on Facebook who analysed Edik's dying words. Thanks too to Pippa Robinson and Suzy McRae, who both grew up in the Snowy Mountains, for their dedicated historical proofreading.

I was lucky to work with two editors on this book: the marvellous Nan McNab and the magnificent

Elise Jones. Between them, they improved this book out of sight with their hawks' eyes for detail and astute emotional intelligence. My gratitude once again to Erica Wagner and the team at Allen & Unwin, who are switched on, committed and, best of all, kind.

All writers get baffled and disheartened sometimes, and Steve Mushin has been there with fantastic advice and unflagging enthusiasm at every stage of every book. To my wonderful family, especially my kids and husband: thanks for always listening to me and believing in me, and for making all my adventures so much better.

If you are one of the wonderful readers who has written me a letter, I give you my biggest and most enthusiastic thanks of all. The Freedom Finders is for you – I hope you continue to enjoy the series!

ABOUT THE AUTHOR

EMILY CONOLAN IS a writer and teacher, who is also known for her humanitarian work. For her role in establishing a volunteer support network for asylum seekers in Tasmania, she has been awarded Tasmanian of the Year, Hobart Citizen of the Year, and the Tasmanian Human Rights Award. The stories of courage and resilience she has heard in the course of her work with refugees, combined with tales from her own family history, inspired her to write the Freedom Finders series.